On

OTHER TITLES IN PAN

Sandy Asher
Everything is Not Enough

Judy Blume
Forever

A. E. Cannon
Cal Cameron by Day, Spider-Man by Night

Maureen Daly
Acts of Love

Lois Duncan
Stranger With My Face
The Eyes of Karen Connors
I Know What You Did Last Summer
Daughters of Eve

Anne Frank
The Diary of Anne Frank

Will Gatti
Absolute Trust

Robert Hawks
This Stranger, My Father

Will Hobbs
Changes in Latitudes

Norma Howe
The Game of Life

Toeckey Jones
Skindeep

M. E. Kerr
Night Kites
The Son of Someone Famous

Norma Klein
No More Saturday Nights

Ron Koertge
Arizona Kid

Ann McPherson *and* Aidan Macfarlane
Me and My Mates

Harry Mazer
I Love You, Stupid!
City Light

Jim Naughton
My Brother Stealing Second

Mary Pope Osborne
Love Always, Blue

Richard Peck
Those Summer Girls I Never Met

Sandra Scoppettone
Happy Endings Are All Alike

Ouida Sebestyen
The Girl in the Box

Marilyn Singer
Several Kinds of Silence

Jean Thesman
The Last April Dancers

Barbara Wersba
Fat: A Love Story (1st in trilogy)
Love is the Crooked Thing (2nd in trilogy)
Beautiful Losers (3rd in trilogy)
Just Be Gorgeous

Patricia Windsor
The Sandman's Eyes
The Hero

ON THE EDGE

Compiled by
Aidan Chambers

PAN MACMILLAN
CHILDREN'S BOOKS

First published 1990 by Macmillan Children's Books Ltd,
a division of Macmillan Publishers Ltd
This edition published 1991 by
Pan Macmillan Children's Books,
a division of Pan Macmillan Limited
Cavaye Place, London SW10 9PG

1 3 5 7 9 8 6 4 2

ISBN 0 330 31983 3

Printed in England by Clays Ltd, St Ives plc

CONTENTS

TOAD IN THE HOLE

Patricia Windsor

Someone was lurking in the woods. She hadn't seen him, just heard his voice. When she jogged the lanes around the farm, he tried to scare her.

At first, she thought it was Jimmy Cory whose father worked the farm for Neil. But she found out all the Cory boys were down with chicken-pox and then she realised the voice was nothing like fourteen-year-old Jimmy's high-pitched twang. It was an older, wiser voice, an intimate voice in tune with the beating of her blood. It knew her name.

'Run for your life, Theo,' it said. 'There isn't much time.'

It could be her imagination, of course. Like the faces she thought she saw in the bathroom mirror. It could be from the trauma. Neil had said she'd been traumatised. And in such a state, you didn't know what you were doing. Or remembering.

She used to sit in St Margaret's Church, soaking up the atmosphere, saying prayers for better grades, dates with boys, praying to be pretty. She went secretly because her friends would laugh but Eileen found out. Eileen said there was a better way to get what you want. All you had to do, Eileen said, was count to five and cast a spell and the spirits were at your command. So she stopped going to church and started counting. Eileen and she got good grades, good seats at the movies, even their periods a week early so they wouldn't be bothered at the beach. But she did not get pretty, and she did not get dates with boys. She felt uneasy. She asked Eileen what sort of spirits were they dealing with and Eileen laughed and said never mind.

One day, Eileen spent three hours in the supermarket, counting to five until the spirits said it was all right to buy a can of Coke. Eileen was taken away to a hospital and the rumour at school was that she cracked up, being such a high achiever. But Theo knew about *five* and the spirits and she was terrified. When would they come for her? She swore off incantations, even wishing on a wishbone. You can't get something for nothing, she realised. She went back to St Margaret's and prayed for protection. But the terrible thing happened anyway.

Afterwards, Neil brought her to the farm. He said it would be good for her, fresh air, and it would be good for Margot, Neil's wife. Neil appointed himself Theo's caretaker. She didn't argue. You can't argue with people who have their minds set on good deeds. Neil was almost an uncle anyway. Her father's best friend. Margot went along with whatever Neil wanted. But Theo knew she would have preferred to be alone with Neil, without Theo mooning about. People were a strain for Margot who sat all day at her typewriter, writing novels and living in another world.

At four o'clock Neil always said, 'Margot, it's time

for your walk,' and Margot jumped, astonished to be called back to reality. 'Oh, ach,' she said in practical Teutonic tones, 'I better change my shoes.' She'd kick off the spiky heels she wore in the house because they made her legs look long and slim, and put on her wellies. Neil treated them like invalids. He took care of them. His two girls, he called them. 'I protect you from the cruel world,' he said. 'People are mostly pains in the ass,' Margot confided to Theo.

One afternoon, it started to snow but she went out to jog anyway. She needed to run. She knew it was symbolic, running away. She took the track behind the Cory house and their dogs set up an alarm. Jimmy Cory and his two brothers, their faces speckled with the chicken-pox, looked out from an upstairs window. She went through the gate and out into the field where they kept the horses in summer. The earth seemed to undulate, sinking into gulleys, rising on to smooth shoulders. She ran across the open field and felt safe only when she reached the enclosure of the woods.

All was quiet. The snow slipped tenderly between the trees. Big flakes clung to her sweat suit. She ran well. She thought of ordinary things. What will Neil make for dinner? Neil drank white wine with his scrambled eggs. His eyes crinkled at the corners when he laughed. Pale blue eyes like watered silk. Theo found it hard to laugh.

'You are like some old toad,' Margot scolded. 'Why do you not make an effort to cheer up?'

This made Neil angry. He reminded Margot that Theo was recovering from a trauma. Margot shrugged. 'Ach, her face will stick in wrinkles and she will be a toad for ever.'

3

Margot's white hands punctured the air as she spoke, like a witch casting spells. Theo looked in the mirror to see how Margot saw her. There was her long pointy face with its brooding eyes and pale lips. Her hair hung around it like a shroud. Margot was efficiently beautiful.

She ran. The day grew dimmer. She lost track of time.

'Fly like the wind, Theo,' the voice said suddenly from the trees.

Her feet slid on the fresh snow. Panic went off like strobe lights behind her eyes.

'Go away!' she shouted to the nearing dark. The snow fell. The air was thick and dead, like a muffler drawn tight around her throat.

No answer. She ran on. Heard the slap of feet running behind her. Afraid to look around. *Because he fears a frightful fiend doth close behind him tread*, she remembered from a poem they'd read in English lit.

'This is private property,' she yelled.

'I know all about you, Theo,' the voice said.

It almost stopped her. Know what? That strange feeling from deep in the pit of her stomach surfaced momentarily. She'd been trying to keep it down, to swallow it whenever it threatened to burp up. A feeling of something awful. Like she'd done something bad. Something she didn't want to admit. Wanted to forget.

I haven't done anything, she told herself, and it is not a demon chasing me to punish me like Eileen. But in spite of it, she began to count the spell. *One, two, three, four, five*. Save me from this and I will be good for ever.

Ahead was the gate, then the long track to the house. The air swirled, cleared, and the night suddenly appeared out of the sky, hard black with stars. If she could reach the lights of the house she'd be safe. One of the Cory dogs was barking its head off. Neil's shape appeared at the window. He will protect me, save me. He doesn't look it, but he's strong. She once saw him pick up an injured buck deer, carry it all the way back to the farm on his shoulders. The deer bled down the back of his shirt.

'Neil . . . ' she started to call, but saw she'd been mistaken. It was Margot at the window.

Margot leaned out anxiously. 'Where have you been such a long time? Neil has gone to search for you.'

'Time got away from me,' she said lamely. She peeked behind her but no one was there.

'Ach,' Margot said and shut the window with a bang.

The day the thing happened was a Sunday. It was an ordinary day. The sun was shining and it seemed like spring although the weather report predicted snow. Her father looked out the window and said, as he always did, that there was no sense in listening to weather reports.

A smell of the roast came from the kitchen where Mrs Hammond was presiding for the afternoon. Theo went upstairs to finish something for school. She'd put it off all weekend. She told the police, over and over, that she didn't remember hearing anything at all. Only her father's voice saying, 'What's he doing here?'

The police kept asking. Was the voice normal? Was it alarmed, afraid?

A shade, she tried to explain. A shade of difference in what might be alarmed or annoyed. She'd paid no attention because then, on that Sunday with the sun shining, it hadn't mattered. She was busy upstairs. The roast was in the oven. Soon they'd eat and she and her father would take a walk. 'Walk off the fat,' he'd say, as he always did, although they were both thin as rails. They'd walk to the park and look at the trees starting to bloom. He'd predict when the first green leaf would unfurl. He'd want her to bet on it and she'd be afraid he was serious and she'd have to give up her allowance for a month. Her father would take her hand every now and then and hold it until he felt the awkwardness between them and let it go. Her father was as shy as she.

The police asked again, 'What did you hear?'

'The quiet,' she told them. 'Only the quiet shrieking in my head.' They looked at her in a funny way. Thought she was off her nut probably. How can you hear silence?

Easy. Like an alarm shrieking, the silence. She went downstairs. She saw. She wondered if the police saw the guilt in her eyes when she told them she couldn't remember what it was.

At dinner, Margot pushed her scrambled eggs back and forth across the plate. She was distracted because she couldn't think of a good ending for her book. Neil had made the eggs because he'd wasted so much time looking for Theo in the woods. He poured himself another glass of wine and raised it in a toast.

'Safe and sound, Theo,' he said. He smiled, looked concerned, smiled again. 'But be careful out there.

Cory told me some vagrant has been sleeping rough in the woods.'

'Vagrant?'

'He means a bum,' Margot said.

'You mean . . . he's really real?' she blurted.

Neil cocked an eyebrow. 'Of course he's real. That's why I went out to look for you. That's why you need to be careful. He's probably harmless, but you never know.'

'You should not run around all over,' Margot admonished.

'Jogging is good for her,' Neil said. 'Exercise clears the mind.'

Margot, not liking to be crossed, snorted and got up to collect the plates.

'You didn't get your walk today because of me,' Theo apologised.

'You make me sound like a dog,' Margot said. 'Anyway, Neil says we don't go out because of the bum.' She dumped the plates, unrinsed, into the dishwasher.

It could make Theo laugh, almost. A vagrant who'd heard her name somewhere – everybody knew it, even in town. She hadn't imagined the voice. She was getting better. She might even remember soon. The police had wanted to hypnotise her, to help her remember but Neil had said they must not do that because it might break the thin thread of her sanity.

They played Scrabble after dinner. Soon, time for bed. In her room she felt safer. The electric clock whirred next to the bed. She put her head close to the whirr and heard it hesitate, then begin again. As if time was uncertain and might stop.

7

Then in the darkness of her dream she was coming downstairs and the silence was making her ears pop and she saw the hand and the blood and her first thought was, Thank God it's only her . . . and then that face. She didn't want to see the face – it was at the window only for a moment and she thought how incongruous it was that her father had been standing there looking out and commenting on the weather and for a crazy moment she wanted to scream, 'There's no sense listening to weather reports.'

In her dream, it snowed and she slid on the snow down into a gulley where the horses were staying for the winter and they nickered at her and butted her softly with their warm moist noses. She felt good for a moment. But only for a moment because then, as she was lying at the bottom of the gulley, warm and snug, she looked up and saw the face again and knew it was standing there in the dark room, staring at her and grinning.

The morning came, dawning brightful with sun streaking off the snow. She sat up in bed and felt grateful. She was awake and dreams were only nightmares. She thought about names. Margot and St Margaret. Was there something hidden there? Should she have heard the hidden meaning in her father's question and rushed down to save him from death? She got up and walked to the window and stared out until her eyes went blind from the glare. Her feet froze on the cold bare floor. Am I guilty? I feel guilty. Because when I saw Mrs Hammond's blood I felt relieved. It's only her, I thought.

There was one thing, she didn't have to go to school. She'd be horribly behind but for now she didn't mind. She was like Eileen, cursed by the demon spirits and convalescing from the trauma. Somehow she didn't much care any more. All that stuff seemed childish and long ago: whispering at the lockers about who was dating whom and what someone wore on Saturday night.

Neil made her oatmeal and she told him she was going out for a jog. Margot was still upstairs, sleeping late, pondering plots.

The Cory boys were over their pox. Jimmy Cory ran after her as she jogged past his house. 'Ayeh,' he said, puffing like a steam engine in the cold. 'Where'd you get them neat sweats?' His eyes gobbled at the pale blue suit she wore and she didn't have the heart to tell him because where she got the sweats was somewhere he'd never get to. Instead, she made conversation about the chicken-pox and he self-consciously fingered the small scabs on his cheek and said he hoped they wouldn't leave scars. She reassured him with tales of her own pox, walking along with him to the school bus-stop. As they waited, stamping snow, their conversation began to dry up.

'Have you seen that man around anywhere?' she asked, anxious to keep talking.

'What man?' Jimmy asked.

'Your father said some vagrant was sleeping in the woods.'

Jimmy shrugged and then looked a little angry. 'I never heard about no vagrant. Nobody ever told me!'

But he's been home in bed, she thought. He

9

wouldn't know. Men in the woods don't run after strong young boys.

'Hey, listen,' Jimmy said, eyeing the road where the school bus was lumbering towards them. 'Hey, I was thinking, I mean, I don't know if . . . would you like to come to the dance with me on Friday night?'

Theo felt herself blush, hot blood rising to the roots of her hair. She hoped he would think it was the searing wind. She felt so sorry for him: for that moment, his face was as pink as hers and he looked sorry too, that he'd said it, but hopeful as a puppy.

'I don't know,' she said, and added in a hurry as his face fell, 'you see, I'm sort of recovering. I'm not sure I can go out at night.'

'That's okay,' he said, relieved. Maybe he had dreaded she'd accept?

'Bye,' she said. She waited until he was inside the yellow bus and it was pulling off, fat snow-treaded tyres crunching on the snow. She felt like his mother.

She didn't feel like jogging now, only walking back to the house through the cold which had suddenly seeped into her lungs and turned them to ice. For the first time since she'd come to the farm she was thinking about what came next. What came after this? When did you recover from a trauma and go back to life again?

They had tuna salad for lunch. Margot said it was a stupid idea because look out the window and just see how cold it was. 'Why do you serve this summertime dish?' she asked Neil.

'It's a luncheon dish,' he said, 'good for summer or winter.'

Theo wished Neil would go away, go off to do some chore. Wasn't he supposed to do chores on a farm? Mr Cory couldn't take care of everything. Why was he always hanging around? Theo wanted to tell Margot something. She didn't know why. In all fairness she should tell Neil because he was her protector and caretaker and Margot was just his wife. But she felt funny about it. It was an intimate thing. Maybe Margot would understand better. Neil had this tendency to say it was all her mental problem. He wouldn't believe her, she realised.

She had to wait until the dishes were done and Margot was about to go back to her study. Finally, Neil put on his coat and boots and smacked his thick gloves and huffed and puffed and said he would go over to the barn. Theo caught Margot at the study door.

'I think someone was in my room last night.'

Margot was not paying attention. She was halfway into the room before the words registered. She spun around and looked astonished. 'Who?'

'Thank you, Margot,' Theo said. 'Thank you for asking who and not saying it was just a bad dream.'

'Even in dreams we need to know who.'

'It might have been a dream, and yet I'm certain it wasn't. Because I have a clue.'

'A detective now,' Margot said, smiling unsurely because this might not be a good joke to make, after the police inquiry and all.

Theo smiled back. 'It's a very small clue, but it means something to me. I always hang my underwear on the doorknob when I get undressed and this morning everything had fallen to the floor.'

11

'This house is full of holes,' Margot said. 'Breezes blow at you from everywhere.'

'My bra has a strong strap. It would take a pretty stiff breeze. But things always fall off when the latch is pulled. You know how these doors are.'

Margot leaned against the study door and looked it over. She crossed her arms and looked down her very straight nose. 'So someone pulled the latch and came in while you were sleeping?'

'Maybe?'

'Or you got up in the night to use the toilet.'

'I don't remember doing that.'

Margot looked at her. Theo looked back. Theo wasn't good at remembering, was she? Theo hadn't remembered the most important detail of that Sunday afternoon: the face of the murderer.

'Never mind,' she said.

'Lie down,' Margot advised. 'No running in the woods today. Act the convalescent you're supposed to be.'

'It's boring.'

'Then I will give you my manuscript to proof-read. You will find all the little typing errors and you will not be bored.'

It was the first time Margot had ever come close to being friendly. Theo shrunk back, afraid to spoil it. The way she'd shrink from her father when he said something intimate. She wanted his love so much and yet she could never bear to hear him put it into words.

'If you'd rather not . . . ' Margot said, turning away.

'No, no, I'll be glad to do it,' said Theo.

12

When Neil came back from the barn he frowned at seeing Theo sitting at the kitchen table.

'No jogging? You shouldn't sit around all day, it's not healthy.'

'I haven't been sitting around, I've been helping Margot.'

Neil scowled more and shooed her out. He had to get busy, he said, to prepare something suitably winterish for their dinner.

'Nothing's too good for my girls,' he said. There was something in the way he said it that wasn't the same. It wasn't like her father saying something affectionate. Theo wondered if perhaps Neil didn't mean it after all.

She finished the manuscript just before dinner. Neil was sequestered and smells were seeping out from under the kitchen door. Theo tapped lightly on Margot's study door and she said, 'Come,' and kept on typing as Theo entered. She lifted a hand only for a moment, to gesture towards the side of the room and Theo brought the manuscript over to the long oak table and put it down. It hadn't been hard to proofread but she was sure she hadn't caught everything. She knew Margot was being kind, not really expecting a professional job. Theo put the manuscript down and was going to creep out when Margot called, 'Get me another ream of paper from the closet, will you?' and when Theo opened the closet door she saw it.

Not that it was unusual or anything. On a farm you had a gun because you went out to shoot rabbits and things, didn't you? It had been the explosion of the gun that made her ears shriek with silence. That's what the police had been expecting her to answer when they asked, 'Did you hear anything?' How could she have forgotten? She stared at the barrel of the gun – a rifle, a shotgun, she didn't know anything about guns; they'd never had a gun in the house. The barrel was shiny, almost oily, and she knew it would be cold to the touch but when her fingers reached out to caress it, the metal was strangely warm.

'The paper, Theo, if you please,' Margot said. The typewriter clacked and Margot's fingers flew. Who have you shot today?

Neil had guns too. Now that she had seen the one in Margot's closet, she was seeing guns everywhere. How had she missed them before? Guns in a glass-doored case in the entry hall and one over the fireplace – but that one was only for show, some old Indian-killing rifle that had been handed down to Neil with the farm and all its lore.

A gun had killed Mrs Hammond. And. Her father. A gun had made her ears ring with the silence of the dead.

The meal Neil prepared was a feast: roast duck stuffed with apples. All kinds of side dishes: mushrooms, cucumber salad, red cabbage. Margot ticked them off on her fingers:

'*Ente mit Apfeln, Pilze, Schmorgurken, rotkohl.*'

'I like *schmorgurken* best,' Theo said, and Margot's stern face softened and they laughed together. Neil put on his scowl again, until Margot kissed him on the cheek and said how good it was of him and Theo shyly did the same. He looked almost like Jimmy Cory had looked, asking her to the dance.

'Safe and sound today, Theo,' Neil said, raising his glass in a toast. 'It's probably best you didn't go jogging today with this vagrant around.'

Theo chewed the crisp skin of duck. 'Jimmy Cory said he never heard of him.'

Neil looked at Margot. 'Cory probably didn't want to alarm the kids.'

'Ostrich,' Margot said and for a moment Theo thought she was speaking German. 'An ostrich buries his head in the sand, yes?'

'You're right, I'll have a word with him. Even though they're boys, they should be warned.'

'Why don't you call the police?' Theo asked.

'Well, I'm sure the Corys have,' Neil said. 'Look, Theo, there's no need to worry yourself about this.'

'But she thinks someone has broken in,' Margot said. 'She thinks someone was in her room last night.'

Neil looked shocked. 'What? Why didn't you say something to me before this?'

'It's nothing, really,' Theo said, feeling her face going scarlet. She glared at Margot. So much for friendship. Friends didn't tell. She hadn't told when they took Eileen away to hospital. Eileen's mother had asked, over and over, 'But why?' And Theo hadn't said a word because it was a secret pact between them.

'Either it's nothing or it's something,' Neil said, angrily. 'Come on, Theo.'

Theo looked down at her plate. Carcass of duck, she thought. Bones. Death.

It was Margot who intervened. 'Don't bully her.'

'Of course. I'm sorry. I know you're under a great strain. Perhaps it was just a dream, Theo? Perhaps we should call that doctor again.'

'I don't need a psychiatrist.'

'Some sleeping pills, maybe.'

'Really, I'm fine. It was a joke. I was only joking when I told Margot. I was bored. There's nothing to do around here all day. That's why I jog. I'm going jogging again tomorrow morning and the heck with bums in the woods.'

Now it was Margot's turn to look betrayed. 'Ach,' she said. 'Children . . . *die Dinger*.'

She and Neil laughed conspiratorially and Theo felt enraged at them.

'What did she say?' she screamed at Neil.

Neil looked only mildly surprised. 'It's all right, Theo, she just called you silly.'

'I'm not silly at all,' she told them, with as much dignity as she could muster, what with her chin greasy from the duck and the pile of bones in front of her. 'In fact, I'm beginning to remember a lot of things.'

'That's good,' Neil said after a moment. His face darkened and he was the one to get up to clear the dishes from the table. Margot kicked off her spiky heels and put her feet up on the opposite chair. She didn't look at Theo as Theo left the room.

She went upstairs early: she didn't want any games of Scrabble with them. Dinger games. But her room was no longer comforting and safe. It had been desecrated. Tonight she would put a chair in front of the door. She'd make a trap of things to fall off with a loud

16

bang if the door was pushed open as she slept. She thought of the gun down in Margot's closet.

Shoot to kill. That's what had happened. Someone had come in through the open sitting-room window and shot Mrs Hammond in the back.

Theo sat on her bed and thought about how she'd felt so guilty. Not because she'd killed Mrs Hammond – had the police ever suspected her? Because she had been relieved. Mrs Hammond was dead – only Mrs Hammond. That was before she had looked in the hallway. That was before she had seen the face in the window.

There were suddenly raised voices downstairs. Neil and Margot having a fight. She'd never witnessed a fight between them. They sometimes said snide things to each other but they never shouted or got really angry. Theo crept out of her room and listened from the top of the stairs. They were talking about her.

'Either she is imagining things or she is right and someone has broken in,' Margot was saying. 'I do not like the idea of someone walking around while we are in our beds asleep.'

'She was imagining it, I told you,' Neil said.

'What makes you so sure?'

'Because there is no way anybody could have broken in here . . . and what for? Just to go into her room? Nothing was taken, the doors were locked in the morning. It had to be imagination.'

'Then she needs a psychiatrist,' Margot said.

'Of course she does. But I want to see if I can help her first. I don't want to subject her to all that. You know what they wanted to do to her. Hypnotism. Drugs.'

17

'It is nice you know what is best.'

'It's the least I can do for him.'

'And he is repaying you.'

'The money is nothing. I'm concerned for Theo. She's like my own daughter in some ways.'

Theo could hear Margot's famous snort. 'Violins will be playing soon,' Margot said. There was silence. Then a door slammed. Margot had retreated to her study.

In the dark, in the night, the demons come. They came for Eileen in the fluorescent glare of the supermarket but for Theo they would come in the night. She was waiting this time, she was prepared. She kept herself awake with pinches, helped by the two cups of coffee she had sneaked from the kitchen when everybody was asleep. Now. Come. And I will see your face.

But the dark kept glaring into her eyes, just like fluorescent lights, the dark slipped out of her vision and she went momentarily blind. And she felt herself slipping into sleep, into the gulley where the horses pushed at her with their warm moist noses. If only I could stay here for ever, if I could be in this dark warm place with the bodies of horses around me.

The latch was pulled and the door began to open. And although she had planned to keep quiet, to feign sleep, she couldn't stop herself from sitting up and shouting, 'Who is it?'

The door closed.

When she gained the courage to get out of bed and walk across the icy floor and look out – there was no one there. The corridor was dim with the ticking of the clocks of sleep. Perhaps she was going crazy after all.

They were sitting at breakfast, Neil and Theo. Margot was still in bed.

'What have you been remembering?' Neil asked.

She cut the bran muffin in two and spread on butter and honey. 'Everything,' she said. She watched his eyes to see what would happen. But they were Neil eyes, blue as watered silk and they seemed only full of concern and love and she thought I am doing it again, I am running away. I love Neil, I have always loved him, I remember.

I remember when I was a small child and my father asked me who my boyfriend was. I was far too small for real boyfriends because I was sitting in his lap and not feeling self-conscious about it at all, and behind his head the sun was coming down in afternoon gold and I said, 'No, I don't want to tell you,' and my father teased me and said, 'Come on, come on, I won't tell,' and wanting to please him I confessed, with shame, 'Uncle Neil is my boyfriend,' and peered at him to see what he would do. And his face changed and he looked annoyed. 'Uncle Neil can't be your boyfriend, he's too old,' her father said and that was that.

I have loved you so long, she wanted to tell him. But of course he was too old and there was Margot and she was only a Dinger schoolgirl of the type suitable for Jimmy Cory to ask to a dance.

'Everything? Are you sure?' Neil asked.

'Yes. Well almost.'

'You know what you must do then, Theo?'

19

She pulled her hand away from him and picked up the muffin.

'You will have to tell the police. They want to know who killed your father.'

'They killed Mrs Hammond first.'

'And then they killed your father.'

'*He* killed my father.'

'Who?'

'The person in the window. It was a he . . . it was only one.'

Neil got up to put more muffins in the microwave. 'And you saw him? You can identify him now?'

'Do you think he only wanted to kill Mrs Hammond? Do you think it was a mistake to . . . to . . . to . . . '

'Your father is dead, Theo.'

'I keep thinking he'll phone me up. I keep thinking all I have to do is go back there and I'll see him. I can't get used to the fact that he isn't here any more.'

'Theo . . . '

'I mean it in a different way, not in the maudlin way people say things like that. I just can't absorb it, you know? He seems here. He seems too real to be . . . dead.'

'We all feel like that . . . '

Theo looked at him, straight into his watery blue eyes. 'I don't think you feel like that.'

Neil laughed nervously. 'Of course. It's not my father. My father died a long time ago.'

'I'm sorry.'

'Don't be sorry. Go for a run, Theo. It will clear the air.'

Outside, the sun was shining. Why was the sun always shining now?

She didn't go right away. She decided to set more
traps. These were subtle traps for daytime to see if
the demon would go through her things, perhaps read
her journal to look for the name of the murderer.
What the demon didn't know was that she had not
yet remembered that. She had remembered the shot
and coming down and seeing Mrs Hammond's bloody
hand and thinking, 'It's all right, it's only her,' and
then she went into the hall and there he was, lying
as if asleep but the pool of blood beneath him spread
like a map of the world and she watched as the con-
tinents seeped into the grey carpet and thought how
Mrs Hammond would be angry to have to clean up
so much blood. Daddy.

By the time she was ready, with her long underwear
and sweat suit on, the sky was deepening into red.
Blood red, but she remembered what she learned as
a child: Red sky at morning, sailors take warning, red
sky at night, sailors delight.

She went through the gate and out into the field
and looked for the gulley where her horses would be
waiting, down in a hole, warm and moist. The woods
beckoned, though, and she couldn't wait any more,
she had to go.

Get me now, she thought. She wanted to say it
aloud but she was too afraid of making a fool of
herself. Jimmy Cory might hear and misconstrue, he
might think she was trying to flirt.

She ran. The snow had packed down in the last
few days and her feet were sure. She ran and waited
to hear his voice. And at last it came.

'Run for your life, Theo. I know all about you.'

21

'What do you know?' she said, still running.

'I know what you've done.'

'Nothing . . . haven't done anything.'

'Oh, I know, Theo. I know your dark thoughts. I know you took the gun.'

'Never.'

'Took the gun and aimed it, shot him through the heart. Shot the life out of him and now he's dead and never coming back, never going to see you again, Theo, gone to hell.'

'You can't hurt me,' she said. 'You're only a spirit. Margot would call you *die Dinger*; you got Eileen but you can't get me because I'm smarter and I've been expecting you. I went back to St Margaret's and I confessed my sins and I don't believe in you any more. If I don't believe in you, you don't exist.'

'I exist, Theo. I'm here. I'm waiting. Come into my arms.'

She ran. She heard the slap of running feet behind her and she was still too afraid to look. To look upon Pan is death.

'I'm coming, Theo. I'll catch you.'

She veered off the lane and into the woods. Tree limbs slapped at her, tried to catch her. She pushed them aside, she felt their angry scratches on her cheeks. She should have run to the gulley, down in the hole with the horses.

It had to be that she'd run to a stop. Out of breath, but still she wouldn't turn around. She knew he was standing behind her and she knew it wasn't a vagrant in the woods, she knew it was him, the one who came that Sunday afternoon with the shining

22

sun, the one who had made the sound of silence in her ears.

'Theo,' he said softly. 'I'm here.'

She turned.

It was him, of course; at that very moment of turning she remembered. It was his face she saw in the window, his blue-eyed lovely face, the face she'd loved since she'd been a child.

Why oh why oh why, she wanted to ask but even in this terror in the dark woods where demons lurked behind every tree and Pan waited with cloven hooves, she was aware of how corny that sounded.

He was the one who asked the question. 'Why did you have to remember, Theo?'

If only I hadn't, she thought, you could stay in my heart for ever, like a demon lover, the murderer of my father.

'I hate to do this,' he said and she almost laughed. What was he going to do anyway? Shoot her with one of the guns from the glass case? They'd know.

He came forward and put out his arms and she wanted to step into his embrace because it was both death and life, to have now what she had always wanted. That's why someone like Jimmy Cory seemed so silly, and that's why she'd been waiting all these years. If Neil wanted her then she must be pretty because Margot was pretty. But, no, she remembered suddenly as his arms went around her, he wants me because he wants me dead.

He was going to strangle her. A love knot, tied with her own scarf. And then he'd say the vagrant did it and some poor old man who never did anyone any

23

harm would get into trouble, just like Mrs Hammond got into trouble. Why did he shoot Mrs Hammond? Because she knew him. Because her father knew him. 'What's he doing here?' her father had asked and now she understood. Her father had never liked Neil. That's why he'd been angry when she said Uncle Neil is my boyfriend. Poor Daddy.

'Come into my arms, Theo,' he said. Seductive was death and she couldn't resist now. He would kill her anyway, even if she ran. He was strong although he didn't look it. Perhaps he would sling her over his shoulder like the buck deer and she would bleed down his back.

But some instinct for preservation made her take a step away. Neil smiled. 'Come on, Theo, there's a good girl. Come to your Uncle Neil.'

She took another step back. From far off, she heard the Cory dogs howling.

The sun was gone. The demons laughed in the trees, or was one of them walking on the crunchy top layer of snow?

'I'm sorry to have to do this,' he said again. He took the ends of her scarf and pulled. She closed her eyes.

I am not afraid, in the valley of the shadow. If Daddy is dead then it can't be so bad, he'd have come back to warn me if it was bad. What I don't like is the idea of not knowing myself any more, not knowing who I am in the cosmos. Will I remember anything at all?

For a moment, before the scarf hurt, she felt sorry for herself, but from a distance. Sorry she had to die so young; now that was maudlin if anything was.

But I am going to die, she thought and she stared straight into Neil's blue eyes. She heard the demons coming behind her. Neil blinked.

There was the blast and then the shrieking silence. Her ears were full of the memory of it and her nose smelled the stink of it. Neil fell, hands still tight on her scarf, pulling her down with him until she fell upon him in a lover's embrace. His blood seeped into the snow. Not the map of the world, just a ragged stain.

Strong hands pulled her off the corpse.

But not before she smelled him, tasted his cheek, knew his skin more intimately than she had ever done in the chaste kisses of the past.

'*Er ist zu bedauern,*' Margot said. 'One must feel sorry for him.'

The gun dropped from her hand and its barrel pierced the snow.

'Come home, little toad,' she said. 'We will do what we have to do.' She put her arm around Theo's shoulder and Theo did not shrink away from the touch, even though she could feel the chill of Margot's fingers through her thick gloves.

They emerged from the woods into the moonlight and Theo saw silver tears on Margot's cheek.

'How did you know?' she asked.

Margot turned towards her with a sardonic smile. 'I am the mystery writer, am I not?' She shrugged and her body sagged. 'Besides, he was away from the farm the day your father died, not here as I told the police.'

'You loved him,' Theo said gently. 'Why save me?'

Margot would not answer. She turned her face

back into the wind and let her tears be blown away.

St Margaret, Theo thought, we have atoned for our sins. She took Margot's hand as they walked up the track to the twinkling lights of the farm.

THE TRAP

Robert Westall

I can't speak of the way Stephanie Harcourt died.

You probably read about it in the papers; I couldn't bear to. She was my neighbour and my friend. And I saw the face of the man who found her dead, and I'll never forget it.

I hadn't seen her for about three days. She often popped in for a coffee, mid-morning. Or around teatime, with a few cakes she'd baked. Or I'd see her round the shops, or out mowing her lawn. She kept busy, because her husband was out in Saudi Arabia. She'd tried living out there, but she couldn't take the heat and the boredom. She said she couldn't live without green grass, and the smell of rain. She was a passionate gardener; my garden is still full of the cuttings she gave me. It's all I have to remember her by. I miss her, being a widow, with children far away. She was ten years younger than me, thirty-five.

I don't know why I didn't miss her sooner. But I was so taken up with my cat, William, who was also missing. And she was always popping off to see her parents in Birmingham, because of being alone so much. Her father had an electronics firm

27

there, very hush-hush. Though she once mentioned computers and artificial intelligence, and another time she said they were working on a new lie-detector for the FBI. The firm must have been doing very well, the presents he was always giving her. Not just hi-fi stuff, like Bang and Olufsen, but marvellous intricate old clocks, antiques that must have cost a fortune. She was an only child. She seemed very fond of her parents.

The first hint of trouble was Tom, our milkman. He knocked on my door, because two days' milk had piled up on her step. Tom takes his duties seriously, with people who live alone. He saved the life of one old woman down the village, who was lying helpless after a stroke. And Tom was a worrier.

I'm afraid I pooh-poohed him, rather. Stephanie was always the picture of health. She swam, and played tennis twice a week. And we weren't a worrying sort of district; a large village full of big old houses, and no council estates full of the unemployed within ten miles. People were still a bit sloppy about locking their doors, then. We didn't even have a Neighbourhood Watch Scheme.

I told Tom not to worry; she must have forgotten to cancel the milk. I even asked him to keep an eye open for William. Then I went and collected the milk off Stephanie's doorstep. It was a beautiful morning in June, and her lawn was just beginning to re-sprout daisies. Somehow, that convinced me she must be away; she was very regular with the lawn-mower. I remember how nice the sun looked on her front door. There was no hint of what lay behind it. The first day's milk had gone off, pushing the cap up with a column of clogged sour cream. But the second day's was usable. I hate waste.

As I was picking up the bottles, my cat William came strolling home, looking as pleased as Punch with himself.

That was the last good news I had for a long time. The next thing was a ring on my front doorbell. Ring, ring, ring. I stamped down the front hall calling, 'All right, all right. Where's the fire?'

I opened the door, and a very young policeman was standing there. Swaying. Holding himself up with one hand on my ornamental urn. His face was so white that his freckles stood out like bloodspots. He was staring at something over my left shoulder. He moved his lips and nothing came out. I helped him into my lounge, thinking he'd been taken ill. He fell into my sofa, then suddenly bent over and was sick all over my Persian rug.

I still couldn't get any sense out of him. He just went on staring and shivering. So I reached for my cordless phone, and dialled 999 and reported a policeman in distress. Even then, I was ironically amused. The rug was probably ruined, but insured. I was already shaping the whole thing into an amusing story for the tennis-club . . .

Half an hour later, an inspector came round to put me in the picture. A much older man. I would have said a hardened man except that his mouth, too, had fits of trembling as he spoke.

The young policeman had been our new beat-constable. Keen to make good. Tom the milkman had met him on his rounds, and mentioned the bottles

29

of milk. Having nothing better to do, he'd decided to check up. Knocked on the front door, then gone round to the back. Found it swinging. Walked in and found . . .

It was only by the grace of God it wasn't me that found her. I'd meant to nip round the previous night, only I'd spent too long looking for William instead. Me worried about William while Stephanie lay . . .

It was the way she must have had to suffer. In silence, with that ragged chewed bloody gag in her mouth. All those hours, with only a brick wall between her and me. With the soothing sounds of the village coming in to her ears. Mr Jenkins cutting his hedge, lawn-mowers, the fish-man slamming his van doors.

As the Inspector got up to go, I asked whether I'd be able to see her, later, at the Chapel of Rest, to say goodbye. The Inspector tightened his lips and shook his head silently. Nobody would ever see her again, except the one who identified her and the forensic experts. Somehow, that made her doubly lost. I kept seeing her face, smiling at me. Her hands delving lovingly into the earth of her garden.

I cried a long time. Before I realised that the murderers might have come to my house instead.

They never caught anybody for it. There were bloody handprints on the wallpaper, but they didn't match anything in the police records. A lot of her nice things were taken, small antiques and jewellery. But they never turned up anywhere. That was the worst thing, in a way. That they'd been cool enough to walk off with her things, after what they'd done to her.

I don't know how I lived through the next two weeks, next to that empty house. Like everybody else in the village, I invested a fortune in locks and bolts. One day I counted four vans from security firms in our road alone. Down in the village, husbands were actually nailing up back doors and screwing thick plywood over back windows. Half the women were on the verge of a nervous breakdown. There was wild talk of enrolling wives in the local pistol-club. One farmer's wife nearly blew off her own husband's head with a shotgun. Only her hands were shaking so badly she blew a great hole in the ceiling instead.

It was impossible to sleep, until dawn and the first passing traffic. You can fit the best locks and bolts in the world, and in the middle of the night they seem no better than bits of wet paper. And all day the phone ringing. Women friends and neighbours. 'Are you all right? Are you all right?' But every time the phone rang, you thought something else terrible must have happened.

In the end, after I had watched Stephanie's husband go out through the front gate with the police, I took myself and William off to my daughter's in Portsmouth for a while. I never saw a man with a face so ruined. I knew he'd never get over it. He went off back to Saudi, to live as he could.

When I came back from Portsmouth, her house was up for sale. So were three other houses in our road. But there didn't seem to be any buyers. Or I'd have put my own on the market.

And Stephanie's garden, her lovely garden, went to wrack and ruin. The grass of her lawn grew knee-high. The privet hedge grew like a forest,

31

as if the house was crouching in terror behind it.

I think I might have gone out of my mind, for sheer lack of sleep. Until, one lunchtime, waking doped with sleeping pills, I looked out of my bedroom window and saw a furniture van standing at the gate of Stephanie's house. I thought at first they'd come to take the last of her furniture away. But no, they were carrying stuff in. And there was a stranger, a white-haired man in a suit, telling them where to put it.

That was the first time I saw Mr Megstone.

All I felt was rage, that anyone could be so inhuman as to want to live there.

Then I wondered if he'd come from a long way off, and didn't know what had happened in the house. Maybe the damned house-agent had deceived him . . .

But surely he'd seen the blood-splashes on the walls? The bloody fingerprints?

Maybe they'd redecorated . . . I struggled desperately with myself, to be fair to the white-haired man. After all, he looked old, and there was something rather frail in the way he moved.

I heard a gentle tapping on my front door, well before dusk. The westering September sun was still streaming through my lounge windows. So I went to my front door. Peeped through my new spy-hole.

His face looked weird through the lens: all nose and mouth, and the eyes a long way back. But then everybody looks the same through a spy-hole. You learn to make allowances. Otherwise I thought it was an impressive face. Very intelligent, but very tired. As if he'd lost nearly as many nights' sleep as I had. Not days' tired, but months' tired. As if he was driving himself just to keep going. Those deep determination marks round the mouth . . .

I hadn't the heart to insult him by opening the door on the chain. Heart in my mouth, I opened it fully. After he'd said who he was, and we'd shaken hands, I asked him in for a cup of tea. That was the funny thing about Mr Megstone. I liked him at first sight. Even now that I know the appalling things he did, even now I've seen the graves, I still think of him sadly.

But that was long afterwards. That day, we talked gently over a cup of tea. I kept having the odd feeling I'd met him somewhere before, that his face, some of his gestures, seemed familiar. I asked him whether he'd ever lived locally. He said no, he'd lived in the Midlands all his life. He'd just retired, and this seemed a nice part of the world. He was a widower, with no children, so he could please himself.

The big question kept coming up into my throat, like a lump of unswallowed food. I couldn't bear not to ask it. Finally I said, 'You know . . . what happened next door?'

He closed his eyes, as if a spear had gone straight through him. 'Yes,' he said. 'Poor soul. I hate to think how she must have suffered.' Then he said, very humbly and apologetically, 'The house . . . was very cheap. And I had to have somewhere to live.'

'Yes,' I said gravely. Almost mimicking his slow gentle tone.

'It's not the house's fault,' he said. 'The house is

not to blame. It must have been a lovely house, before it all happened. She had such . . . lovely taste . . . in wallpapers and curtains and carpets.'

I shuddered, thinking about the wallpaper in that bedroom.

'I'm keeping that room locked up,' he said. 'I use it to store things.'

I shuddered again. What a strange thing to do. Every time he went in, he would see the bloodstains. But he was running on, gently.

'The garden was lovely, too. I shall try to get her garden back as it was. I think she would've wanted that, don't you?'

It seemed to me then, for a second, that he spoke a little too familiarly of her, as if he, some time, had known her. Then the thought got lost, because I started to cry, remembering her in her garden. It seemed a lovely thing to want to do, restore her garden. I dried my eyes, after a moment, and said so.

'You must have been very fond of her,' he said. 'I think she was very fond of you.'

'How can you know that?' Again, suspicion twitched in me.

He gave his weary smile. 'Just guessing. Two nice women, living alone, next door to each other.'

It wasn't until long after he'd gone that I asked myself how he'd known I lived alone.

But as the days passed, my suspicions faded. He was an attractive man to talk to, over the garden fence. And I was grateful that, as I watched him slowly and painfully putting Stephanie's garden to rights, his stooping figure began to erase the memory

34

of her stooping figure. In some ways, his slow stooping patience reminded me of her slow stooping patience. And when, in October, he offered me some geranium cuttings, I could have wept. Stephanie had always offered me cuttings then.

It baffled me, trying to guess how old he was. I had thought him nearing seventy when I first met him. But, moving around the garden, his body seemed younger than his face. He seemed to have lost a lot of weight recently. His frame was broad, though thin, and his clothes tended to hang on him, as if made for a bulkier man. But he moved as gracefully and loosely as a boy. Far from nearing seventy, I guessed he must be nearing sixty. Some hidden grief had lined his face, and made him hesitant. And nothing attracts a foolish unattached woman like a sense of hidden tragedies in a man. Especially a man with such a lively curious mind as Mr Megstone. Talking over the back fence, his mind was into everything, with the curiosity of a boy, and the sureness of a man who has once held power. I wondered what he'd been, because he was clever with his hands, too; he mended my misbehaving lawn-mower, that I'd put in for repair four times in six months; and it has never misbehaved since.

I wondered why he'd retired early, and what from, but my careful questions got me nowhere. 'Trade,' he would say, 'vulgar trade. Factories, dividends, filthy lucre. Isn't this a lovely rose-tree? I hate trimming them when they're still blooming . . . '

'That was her favourite,' I said suddenly, tears in my eyes.

'Yes,' he said gravely, as if he'd known her all her life.

*

When he gently asked me to tea, I took a deep breath and went. It wasn't quite as painful as I'd expected. He hadn't changed any of her decoration, and most of the curtains and carpets were the same. But she'd always kept them plain and simple, and now they were sort of . . . lost . . . behind all his own furniture. Beautiful furniture, pictures, all antiques and *what* antiques! There must've been hundreds of thousands of pounds worth. The sort of stuff you don't see nowadays, outside of stately homes.

'I hope you've got good burglar-alarms,' I said. It started as a joke, till I remembered we'd all had our burglar-alarms fitted since Stephanie died.

'No burglar-alarms,' he said, almost gaily.

'But you've got good locks and window-catches . . .'

'No,' he said, 'I'm too old for all this newfangled stuff. If burglars come, they'll get in anyway. They just do more damage getting in, that's all.'

'But suppose they do break in?'

'If they come, they come. All the stuff's insured. Have another sandwich!'

I looked at him curiously. I'd got to know him pretty well by that time. I confess, I was strangely attracted to him. In spite of his deep underlying sadness. Perhaps because of it. He had an air of someone going inevitably to his doom, and not really caring. Gay, almost, at times with a kind of gallows humour. But this wildness of talk about burglars . . . as if he would almost welcome them . . . it seemed very wrong. I did not want it. I wanted to turn his gallant autumn back into a brief spell of

36

summer. Indian summer, anyway. He had told me, in a rare moment of confidence, that he was fifty-seven. I was forty-six by then. It didn't seem an unbridgeable gap. A few happy contented years, on the brink of eternity . . . Of course, now I shudder. But I didn't know *anything* then.

We changed the subject, to the American dollar crisis and my falling capital. He certainly didn't seem in the least interested in my money; but he gave me a few bits of shrewd financial advice that I was glad later that I'd followed.

As I left, I noticed a wall-clock in the hall. A small beautiful clock, all intricate fretting and two shining brass weights.

'How strange,' I said. 'That's just like the clock that Stephanie had, the one they stole . . . after . . . '

For once, he looked suddenly guilty. Was lost for words. But he came back smoothly, 'A Viennese regulator. Very fine clocks. They're getting rather rare in this country now . . . '

Two odd things happened, after that. The first was the van outside his door, marked:

NEWTON AND TONGS. METAL FABRICATORS

From the van's interior, two men with aprons carried a series of heavy steel plates, with holes drilled in them at regular intervals. And when I say heavy, I mean heavy; the two men were staggering as they carried them. All that day, there came a sound of drilling and hammering inside his house. I thought he had taken my advice about burglars to heart very seriously indeed. But then the men and the van went away, and the next time he had me to tea, there was no sign of steel plates anywhere. I just supposed that somewhere hidden, he'd built himself a strongroom. But what good was a strongroom, with antiques on display all over the house, and the locks and bolts no better than before?

The other odd thing he did was to sell that Viennese regulator soon after. He advertised it in all the local papers, among the adverts for Victorian fireplaces and modern vinyl three-piece suites:

ELDERLY COLLECTOR WISHES TO SELL
FINE EARLY VIENNESE REGULATOR. £700
FOR QUICK SALE.
APPLY MEGSTONE, ARLEY VILLA,
RADDON GARDENS, SOUTHWICK.

The implications horrified me. I went round to see him in a rage, the newspaper still in my hand. And I was sharp with him.

'Are you *asking* for trouble? Letting all the local burglars know you've got that kind of stuff, and that you're elderly into the bargain? Are you asking to have your house done over? You haven't got a burglar alarm, and not a decent lock in the place . . . you bloody old fool.' Then I burst into tears.

He listened to me in silence, then gave me a clean and beautiful white handkerchief, to wipe my tears away with. I looked up at him, very shyly, in the end. His face was concerned for me, but inexpressibly sad. And stern.

'My life is my own, Marjorie,' he said. 'I have grown fond of you, and perhaps you have grown a

38

little fond of me. But that does not give you rights over my life. I must do as I think best.'

I was put out. Badly put out. It was as if he'd looked straight into my heart, and seen what was there, and gently rejected it.

I blundered out of the room. Anything to get away from those gentle understanding eyes. I was in such a state that in the hall I opened the wrong door: the door that led under the staircase.

'Not that way,' he said, very sharply. 'You don't want to see my domestic squalor.' And led me to the front door by the arm. And asked me whether I was all right, before he let me go home.

At home, I flopped on to my couch as hopelessly as the young constable had, all those weeks ago. But I wasn't sick; with me it was just tears. It was only after I had stopped crying that I began to wonder about the sharp tone in his voice, as he had led me away from that doorway under his stairs.

Somehow, the tone had been wrong. It was not a tone of male embarrassment.

It had been a tone of fear.

As I said, he sold the clock. Two weeks later, he advertised and sold a fine bronze statue of Venus, for a thousand pounds. Then it was a pair of gilt candelabra. The local newspaper finally cottoned on to what was happening and sent a photographer and reporter to interview him, and report on his collection. It was featured in a double-page spread. Including the fact that he thought burglar-alarms were not much use. Then he got featured in the county magazine . . .

I tried several more times to reason with him.

Without result. Finally, in despair, I called in Jim Connor, our local beat-constable. Jim was the one who had found Stephanie. I gave him the mug of tea that no policeman in his right mind refuses, and studied him.

He had not yet got over finding her. His considerable boyish charm seemed to have gone for ever. He was paler than I remembered him, and his right eyelid flickered from time to time, in an uncontrollable tic. But he seemed to be coping. There was a new discipline about him; and a caring. He had worked very hard to reassure us, since the murder, especially those of us who were living alone. Everyone spoke very highly of him; we had grown close to him. I thought he would make an excellent superintendent one day, intelligent and wise. If his nerve held out long enough.

I told him of my worries for Mr Megstone. To my surprise, his face lightened.

'I think you're worrying unduly, Mrs Fletcher. Mr Megstone might seem frail, but I think he can handle himself.'

I said sharply that I thought he was being unduly optimistic.

He leaned forward and said, 'Can I tell you something in confidence?'

I said I thought I could be trusted.

He took another sip of tea and said, 'I was on the early shift, about a month ago, when I came across Mr Megstone standing at his gate. He had a lad with him, a big rough lad in torn jeans I didn't like the look of, at all. Except he stood beside Mr Megstone very humbly, with his head down. Mr Megstone said

40

he had caught the lad trying to break into his house. He'd had a good talk with him, and the lad had seen the error of his ways. In fact the lad had confessed to several other burglaries he had done, and now he wanted to go to the police-station and make a clean breast of everything.

'I looked at the lad, incredulous. But he just glanced up, in a flinching sort of way like he was terrified of me, and nodded without a word.

'So I said all right, I'd take him in. And did Mr Megstone want to charge him with breaking and entering as well? Mr Megstone just laughed and said, "Well, he found my back door open, and he hasn't taken anything or done any damage, so I'll let him off this one. He's in enough trouble without me. Aren't you, Ronnie?"

'And the lad just nodded, with his head down. So I took him in, and he sang like a canary. We cleared up quite a lot of burglaries . . . The lad just seemed brain-washed . . . Didn't give a bit of aggro.'

'That's all very well,' I said. 'But the next one mightn't be so soft . . . '

'It might surprise you to know, Mrs Fletcher, that it's not the first time it's happened. If Mr Megstone keeps it up, my arrest-record will be so good they'll have to promote me to sergeant.'

'I don't believe it, Jim. It's against nature.'

'Oh, it's all true. Times, dates, modus operandi. We've recovered a lot of stuff. Super's very pleased.'

'I don't mean that. I mean . . . how is Mr Megstone doing it?'

Jim shrugged uncomfortably. 'Dunno. Maybe he's

a retired preacher. Maybe he gives them religion.' He was trying to laugh it off.

'Poppycock,' I said.

'I never look a gift-horse in the mouth,' he said.

We parted; not in a very good temper with each other.

An unease grew between me and Mr Megstone; a constraint. We still spoke to each other over the garden fence. But without warmth. Still, I confess I continued to watch him, as he came and went, and worked in his garden. And I watched that house more closely than I've ever watched anything in my life. Maybe Mr Megstone did feel he had a holy mission to reform burglars. But his adverts in the paper began to have the nasty look of the outer filaments of a spider's web. They sickened me. Burglars are not animals, to be snared for a hobby.

Anyway, I noticed immediately when Mr Megstone went missing. One fine morning, he was not out working in his garden. I shopped at my usual time, and did not see him going round the shops. Coming home, I tapped on his front door. *That* front door. It looked so very much as it had on the morning I collected Stephanie's milk from the step . . . There was a pint bottle on his step now.

No answer. I managed to get myself through lunchtime; telling myself he might have gone into Manchester for the day, and that I was not his keeper. But I tapped on his door again at two. Still no answer. And the milk was still there. I drove into Manchester myself, and did some pointless shopping, because I was quite unable to sit still.

I returned at dusk. There were no lights on in his house, and the milk was *still* there. I was so terrified that I hadn't the courage to park my car in the garage round the back. I scarcely had the courage to let myself into my own house. I put on the light in the hall, and rang the police-station. All the time imagining what might once again lie behind my wallpaper and that innocent brick wall.

I asked for Jim by name. He was, as luck would have it, on the beat that night. They asked if it was urgent, and I said no, lying in my teeth. It was just that I'd like a word with my friendly neighbourhood bobby. It's funny, no matter how terrified you are, you're still more terrified of being thought a fool by policemen.

They said they'd radio him and get him to call, as soon as was convenient.

I'm glad to say he was round in a remarkably short time. I think he knew something was up.

'Mr Megstone's . . . missing.'

'Since when?'

'I haven't seen him since yesterday teatime – he was working in his garden. I've been knocking on his door all day. He's not in. The milk's still there.'

He looked at me, exasperated on the surface; but there was fear underneath. 'That's ridiculous. He might have gone to Manchester and stayed on for the pictures. It's only half past seven now!'

'He's never away. I don't think he has anywhere he wants to go to. I see him every day. If he was going anywhere, he would've told me.' My voice rose to a wail. I knew I was sounding childish.

'Sorry. There's nothing I can do. There's nothing I

can tell the duty-inspector. I have no *grounds* . . . '

'Be damned to your grounds,' I said. 'If you don't
do something, I won't stay in this house tonight.
I'm taking William and going to my daughter's. And
I'll be obliged if you'll wait and see me off the
premises.'

He put on his be-reasonable act. 'I know what
you've been through, Mrs Fletcher . . . '

'Then *do* something about it.'

He hesitated. Then grinned. A nice grin, but weary.
'I'll knock on his door. I'll check round the back.
You'll have to be satisfied with that.'

It was a start. I locked up my house, leaving
all the lights on, and we went.

No answer to his knock. Mr Megstone hadn't drawn
his lounge curtains, and I could see the backs of his
chairs, by the distant streetlight.

He knocked again, then said, 'Okay, we'll try the
back.'

And went off very quickly, shining his lamp here
and there, over Stephanie's plants.

He stopped; said abruptly, 'The back door's open.'
There was a slight tremor in his voice; he was remembering the other time.

My head spun, and I had to put one hand against
the wall to stop myself falling.

'Now I've got grounds to enter.' The official heavy
tone was back, but it couldn't quite hide the fear.
'Shall I take you home first?'

'No, I'll come with you.'

'Probably nothing. He probably went out and forgot
to shut his back door.'

Neither of us believed him. I saw him reach inside

and click the light-switch. The light didn't come on. He turned his pale face to me, a blur in the gloom.

'Odd.' I saw his dim hand reach for the radio clipped to his tunic. But it fell away again. Like me, he was afraid, but more afraid of making a fool of himself, radioing in about nothing.

He made up his mind with an effort, and pushed on into the kitchen. Shone his torch around. Nothing but Mr Megstone's familiar kitchen things, kettle, mixer, two plates and a bag of flour on the red formica table-top. With their shadows fleeing away behind them, strangely, in the light of the torch.

'Nothing here, then.' There was a slight catch of relief in his voice, like a death-sentence postponed. He pushed the door open, into the hall.

There was a streak of light on the left. In all the darkness, just one streak of light.

'That's the door under the stairs,' I said.

The door Mr Megstone had got scared about when I went to open it.

'Be careful,' I said, pointlessly.

He swung that door open.

'Good God!' But it was incredulous relief in his voice, nothing worse. 'Look at this!' He plunged down inside.

I followed, and looked where he had gone.

A small room, dimly and goldenly lit. A chair on each side of the door: upright, ugly steel chairs, incredibly strong-looking. But I hardly spared them a glance. For the whole far wall of the tiny room was a showcase. A glowing showcase full of the most magnificent jewellery display.

'Must be worth a fortune,' he said, breathless.

Breathless with expecting a corpse, and finding a king's ransom.

I went to follow him; there were three steps down. But it wasn't the steps that made me hesitate; it was a dark two-inch groove across the threshold, under my feet, a seemingly bottomless groove . . .

I hesitated because I couldn't think what such a groove should be for. But I only hesitated for a moment, then I stepped down after him.

'One of these cabinet doors is open,' he said. And reached up to it; whether to close it or not I will never know.

For as he moved it, there was a downward movement at my back; I felt the swift draught of its passing before I heard that terrible clang.

I whirled round, and where the doorway had been was a solid steel plate, thick with rust and grease. Without hinge or handle. Now I knew what the groove across the threshold had been for; and the metal fabricators. A steel plate that had dropped like a guillotine.

We were caught like rats in a steel trap.

For behind the innocent floral wallpaper the walls were steel; and under the white vinyl paint, the ceiling was steel; and under the soft thick green carpet, the floor was solid concrete.

'Neat,' said Jim viciously, as he gave up lifting the carpet and tearing off wallpaper, and probing the ceiling with his clasp-knife. 'A rat-trap for burglars. And jewellery for bait. The old sod must be out of his mind. He'll get two years for this. I'll have his guts for garters . . . '

He clicked on his radio. His hand was trembling, but his voice was steady, while he called the police-station.

Until the station didn't answer. Or rather, answered with a blurred and useless crackle. 'Too much brick and steel around us,' he said. 'If I can't hear them, they certainly can't hear me.'

It was in the helpless silence that followed that the other voice came. It made us both jump. But, thank God, it was Mr Megstone's voice. Though very calm and cold.

'Listen carefully. The room you are in is almost airtight. Your air supply is strictly limited. You have enough to last about an hour.'

I glanced around wildly.

Jim nodded to a corner. 'Loudspeaker behind that grille.'

'It's all right. It's Mr Megstone,' I said. Then, like a trusting child I called out, 'Mr Megstone? It's me. Mrs Fletcher. There seems to have been some kind of mistake. We came because we were worried about you.'

'Cheshire police here, sir,' said Jim in his direst tone. 'I would advise you to release us immediately. Or else you could be in very serious trouble.'

We waited, rather anxiously. It is not a pleasant sensation to be trapped in a steel box, even when you think help is at hand.

But when the voice did come, it repeated the same message. About the air supply. In the same cold manner. With exactly the same intonation. Like the voice of the Speaking Clock. Or the voice on the Tube that tells you to stand clear of the doors.

47

There is no mercy in a tape-recording. Any more than there is in steel walls. We waited; at the mercy of a dead machine.

You will have proved by your exertions that there is no way out of this room. Except one. By answering my questions. Please take your seat in one of the chairs provided. Again, I repeat, your supply of air is limited to one hour.

'Do as it says,' said Jim. He was still in control of himself at that point. 'Humour it. I think it's our only chance.'

Helplessly, I sat down. The steel seat of the chair was icy cold. It seemed to be made of three-inch steel girders. And it didn't move as I sat in it, like an ordinary chair; I guessed it was bolted to the floor.

Put your ankles and wrists in the clamps provided.

I looked down. On the arms and legs of the chair were stainless steel clamps, open like the claws of a crab; thicker than handcuffs. Once they closed round my wrist or ankle . . .

You now have fifty minutes of air left.

'Do as it says, for Christ's sake,' said Jim. There was sweat dripping down his face. He pressed his wrists and ankles into the clamps, and they closed smoothly round him, with tiny clicks. 'I'll put this old bastard away for life, when I lay my hands on him.'

That cheered me, somehow. Enough to put my

48

own wrists and ankles into the clamps. When the cold bands closed around me, I could have screamed my head off. Then I noticed the yellow wires running up the chair. Electrical wires. The whole thing suddenly reminded me of an electric chair I'd seen in a TV programme about American prisons.

Good.

There was something horrible about that mechanical approval with its slight hiss and crackle. And my cringing gratitude for it.

Good. I must warn you that you are now attached to a lie detector. If you tell lies, the moisture content of your skin will rise and I will know you are lying. Do not tell lies. I do not wish to punish you needlessly. Give me your names and addresses.

We did. Jim first, stressing the word 'constable'. Then me. Is it possible to be terrified out of your wits, and yet embarrassed at the same time? I am hopeless even with telephone answering machines.

You must speak more clearly. Do not mumble. You are not making a clear recording.

I tried again, my voice rising to a hysterical squeak. What was so obscene was that I was talking to the voice of my old friend, who gave me geraniums. But so cold, so infinitely cold that it was like a knife through my heart. Where was the *real* Mr Megstone? Why didn't he come and save me?

I will take the male first. Tell me what crimes you have committed over the last six months.

'I haven't committed any crimes,' snapped Jim. 'I'm a *policeman*.'

The next second . . . it was horrible. Blue sparks seemed to grow from his chair. His body leapt and kicked, against the clamps. From a man, he became a dancing dark blue marionette, a flailing blue dummy, not human. There was a strong smell of ozone; and what might have been burning. It seemed to go on and on. I wanted to scream; but I had no breath.

Then, at last, it stopped.

'Jim?'

He moaned. He seemed to have bitten himself, for blood was running down his chin from his mouth. I also became aware of a spreading dark stain between the legs of his uniform trousers.

'Jim? Are you all right?'

'What the hell is going on?' he said, dazed. His voice was like a lost and broken ghost. All the policeman had gone, leaving little more than a terrified animal.

Tell me what crimes you have, committed in the last six months.

He began to gabble. All the peccadilloes of his harmless young life. Going for a pint after duty, when his wife was expecting him home. Sitting in a lay-by, eating toffees, when he should be on foot-patrol. Using the Panda to nip to the shops, wasting police petrol. His vague yen after a pretty WPC. Fiddling his expenses for going on a course. The sins got smaller and smaller, but he seemed too frightened to stop. Until finally he ran dry and wailed, like a child, 'I can't think of any more.'

What were you doing on the afternoon of Friday the fifth of June?

I heard Jim's sharply indrawn breath. That was the day of Stephanie Harcourt's murder.

There was a long and terrifying silence, while he struggled. It's not easy to remember what you were doing, all those months ago. Then at last he cried out, in a burst of boyish relief that made me want to weep, 'I was at a crime-prevention meeting, at Chester. Half a dozen of us went – Sergeant Dewsbury, Len Mostyn – you can ask them.'

You have told the truth. Sit still and be quiet.

I think Jim must have fainted after that. I thought at first he was dead; but then caught his chest moving up and down.

Then it was my turn. I was lucky. I had had time to ponder my sins. Oddly, it reminded me of the time I was a girl, and my parents were High Church, and I had to go to confession once a month. Now I poured out my sins in an endless flood. Spite on the tennis-club committee. Malicious gossip. Taking advantage of the local garage, when

51

they undercharged for petrol. I could not but be
drearily shamed by the utter pifflingness of it all; I
was glad Jim couldn't hear it. But I kept on ramming
them down the cursed machine's loudspeaker . . .

Enough.

Then came the question about the dreadful Friday.
'I did my ironing. And looked for my cat.'

You have told the truth. Sit still and be quiet.

The silence went on and on. Jim groaned, and came
back to himself. 'For Christ's sake, where's Megstone?
Why doesn't he come and release us?' He looked at
his watch, craning his neck. 'The bloody hour's up.
The air'll be . . . '

There was a click from the loudspeaker. At the
same moment the clamps opened. And with a long
painful rumble, the steel door slid up. We looked
out, expecting to see Megstone.

All we saw was darkness. A darkness we got out
into, pretty sharp; though Jim could hardly walk, and
I practically had to carry him.

'Where is he?' he kept mumbling. 'Where is he? I'll
kill the old bastard. I'll see they lock him in the
loony-bin and throw away the key. Who does he think
he is? Who does he think he *is*? God Almighty?'

It was terrible, feeling the hate and rage running
through that weak and shaking body.

'I think he was Stephanie's father,' I said. 'Come
to avenge his daughter. Come to catch the men who

murdered her. Like rats in a trap. Stephanie said her father lived in the Midlands, like Mr Megstone. And her father's firm was working on a new lie-detector for the FBI . . . '

'What do you mean, he *was* Stephanie's father? Where is he now?'

'I think he's dead. Upstairs. Can't you smell that smell? No? Well, I used to be a nurse . . . I think he's dead but he didn't switch things off. That's why it caught us. That's why he didn't come to help us . . . '

But I don't think he was really listening. He was yelling down his radio to the police-station, and getting an answer now. So I picked up his big torch, where he'd left it by the door of that room, and slowly made my way upstairs, to find my old friend.

He lay peacefully on his bed, quite cold. From the icy feel of his hand, he'd been dead some time. But, oddly, there was a smile of utter contentment on his face. He had lain down fully clothed. And he was caked with clay. Not soil, clay. Clay caked on his trousers, well above the knees. Clay caked on his shoes. Clay on his hands. Clay all over the blue bedspread, and clayey footprints on the bedroom carpet.

What had he been doing, to be digging so long and so deep? I thought I knew. I went to the bedroom window, and opened it on to his beloved back garden; her beloved back garden.

There was a spade, standing upright in the earth. And the soil of two of her rosebeds had been disturbed. In long patches.

Patches six feet long and two feet wide.

All that excitement, and dragging and digging must have brought on some kind of heart-attack that had killed him.

But he must have died a happy man.

Stephanie Harcourt had been avenged.

AIR PRESSURE

Jan Mark

You could set it to music, really you could; what do they call it? Plain Song, antiphon, one of those church dirges that make you think God gave up listening hours ago.

Gran: 'Have you got your ticket? Have you got your passport? Don't forget your travellers' cheques.'

Grandad: 'If anything goes wrong you can ring us and reverse the charges.' (Like while over the Atlantic, for instance.)

Khalid: 'Have you got the books?' For the tenth time.

And:

For the tenth time I tell him, yes, of course I have the books. I packed them yesterday. And now, Lord, let thy servant depart in peace et cetera . . .

'Ah, but where did you pack them?'

'In the suitcase, I told you. You don't think I've *un*packed them, do you?'

'We know what happens to suitcases, don't we?' Khalid says. Some nerve, coming from him. What I did with the suitcase on Swindon station is a family joke, nothing to do with Khalid. I suppose he got it

55

from Laura. He isn't family yet, and knowing Laura it's quite likely he never will be. In any case, family jokes are not funny, especially in a family such as ours, which gets around, spreading information like an infectious disease. You never know where it will break out next. Even quite intimate details come back at you courtesy of people like my mother's aunt in Australia who duplicates a kind of newsletter four times a year and circulates it around our far-flung relatives, so that everybody knows how the lettuces are coming up in Melbourne and what Betty and Dave (Mum and Dad) are doing in Singapore, and what I did with the suitcase on Swindon station.

Fortunately Khalid is not seeing me off at Heathrow or he would still be blathering on about books and suitcases up as far as Passport Control. By the time we arrive, I wish no one is seeing me off. I wish I had got the coach to London, the Piccadilly Line to Heathrow and then a baggage trolley; anything better than Grandad miscalculating the time as per usual and getting stuck on the M25. When we do arrive, with Grandad building up for a coronary and Gran having the vapours, we are late for checking in and there is a great long queue at the TransAt desk. I know that if I have to wait even five more minutes with these two registering ninety on the Richter Scale I shall lose my cool, like spectacularly, so I persuade them to go away, at least while I am queuing. People like Gran ought not to be allowed within ten miles of airports; her bad vibes could seriously interfere with the radar. Gran has got to sixty-three without ever flying anywhere. She will be first through the Channel Tunnel. If God had meant us to fly, Gran says, he'd have given us parachutes.

So here I am at the end of the line for London – Toronto, the *very last* person to check in, by the look of it. Of course, no seats left in non-smoking, tourist class. I'm not a tourist, I feel like saying; I am visiting a relative, but all the same I get the last available seat, up at the back in the tail. Is that the bit that drops off first? I shall not tell Gran.

'Just one or two questions, for security,' says the girl at the desk, as my suitcases trundle away over the rollers. 'Are you carrying luggage for anyone else?'

Oh, sure. Look at me, two suitcases, flight bag, handbag, camera, raincoat. Carrying luggage for anyone *else*? Do me a favour.

'Has anyone approached you to deliver a parcel or a letter?'

Vision of stealthy type in dark glasses, sidling from behind a pillar. 'Carry my bomb, lady?'

Back to Gran and Grandad, full of plans to get through Passport Control almost immediately and relax in the Duty Free Shop. Even the Duty Free Shop at Terminal Three is more relaxing than sitting about in an empty room with Gran. Fortunately there is not much time to hang around in. The flight will be called at eleven thirty for take-off at twelve fifteen. No, no, I tell them, I'll go through Passport Control *now* and have a coffee in the departure lounge, to save a last-minute rush. What I do not want happening is what happened last time: Gran going to the bookshop to find me some nice magazines and panicking among the paperbacks which all seem to have pictures of plane crashes on the jackets, flames

57

and debris. I don't know what kind of a nutter stocks those bookstalls. It would put me off, even, and I *like* flying.

So we do our tearful farewells in the middle of a scrum round the telephones where a very old Hindu lady, looking just like Queen Victoria in a sari and wheelchair, is doing a long goodbye with *her* family, about ninety of them. I can't make out who is actually leaving, her or the family. If it is the family they will need a whole aircraft to themselves.

Gran gives me a letter for Laura and I tell her about being approached with requests to carry packages, and then I have to tell her why, which sets her off again, but at last I am on the business side of the barrier, me and my hand luggage, passing through the security check, leaving them to worry in peace until take-off. They will have another seven hours after that, to worry until they hear that flight TA002 has landed safely at Lester B Pearson International Airport – or not. That should liven up the home stretch of the M25 no end, and then they can spend the evening wondering if I've got to Vancouver; or not.

Well, we do get called at eleven thirty and being at the back my row is one of the first to board. I did plan to sit next to the window, but no chance of that, thanks to the M25, but at least I am on the side aisle in the narrow bit, only two seats together, next door but one to the window. Thought with my luck I'd have been in the middle of the centre row with screaming three-year-olds who don't like seat-belts either side. Stow hand baggage overhead. Transfer half contents of flight bag into handbag and vice versa, climb on to seat to reach better, step down and stand on small violent-looking lady who has come up underneath. Hope appearances are deceptive – she will be my next-door neighbour in the window seat. Whop! and a weighty hold-all slams into the luggage bin beside my gear. Mrs Margery McKenna, it says on the label. Belfast.

We untangle ourselves and sit down. Mrs McKenna unpacks a handbag the size of a briefcase, which she seems to use as a filing cabinet. I can see that she is one of those people who hoard till-roll receipts and is going to mislay her boarding pass. I go through the contents of the pocket on the back of the next seat; in-flight magazine, menu, sick-bag, safety instructions for 747s – *love* the safety instructions: jolly little strip cartoons of plane crashing on land, plane crashing on water, happy holidaymakers leaping down emergency chutes, fastening life-jackets, plugging into oxygen masks. The girl with the life-jacket is the best of the lot, she has this serene smile and is inflating her jacket with her little finger crooked. She looks as if she is modelling life-jackets on the catwalk, and the only way you can tell she is tossing about in the stormy ocean after descending sharpish from 30,000 feet is by the way her hair is tastefully blowing sideways like in a gentle breeze. The flight magazine lists all the broadcasts available during the journey, also the in-flight movies. I am glad I like reading and hope my book will last out the trip. It's a pity I didn't put Khalid's books into my flight bag. If I got really desperate, say over Greenland, I could sneak open the parcel. Mind you, it is taped up like he suspected I'd do just that, though the wrapping paper is very posh, as if he'd bought it in Harrods. He probably did. Khalid is not short of a bob or two. It's so thick – bulletproof gift wrap.

None of this is very engrossing but it passes the time while the aircraft fills up – and how. Jumbos look quite spacious until you've got all the sardines on board – so I am surprised when Mrs McKenna says, 'I wonder how much longer we'll be sitting here?' My watch says twelve thirty; we should have begun taxiing a quarter of an hour ago. At which moment our gallant captain comes on the air to welcome us aboard TransAt flight 002. Captain Bligh, he says his name is, which I can scarcely credit, and apologises for the slight delay, caused, he says, by increased airport security. We will, he says, be taxiing at thirteen hundred hours.

'What's that in old money?' says Mrs McKenna. 'Increased security? Did you notice any increased security?'

'They asked me if I was carrying anyone else's luggage or letters.'

'That took all of thirty seconds.'

'I've got a letter from my gran,' I confess. 'Do you think I should have told them?'

'Does your gran belong to any illegal organisations?' Mrs McKenna has not met my gran but she clearly knows the score. 'I'm going out to my son's wedding,' Mrs M says. 'Half my luggage is other people's presents.' No prizes offered for guessing that Mrs McKenna is Irish. Suppose one of Mrs McKenna's family . . . that is, people can be pretty unscrupulous about getting loved ones to carry drugs and explosives. However; 'I wrapped everything myself,' Mrs M continues, 'and made everybody write out their gift tags and then I stuck them on. After all, I said, I'm the one who'll be carrying this lot. I only hope to God I got the right tags on the right gifts. Give him a cheque, I said; what makes you think Liam won't be able to buy matching avocado dishes in Toronto, but, oh no, that would have taken all the fun out of it for them. I hope he's developed a taste for avocados since he went out there, so I do. He's got sixteen of the bloody things.'

I don't know if Mrs McKenna is anxious about flying but I can see she wants to talk, and that is fine by me, because if we don't talk I'll be starting to read my book which is meant to last all the way, not just to Toronto, having extracted the last microgram of excitement from the flight mag and the safety instructions.

And I want to make amends. She doesn't know that I thought about terrorists because she's Irish, but I shouldn't have.

'Does Liam live in Toronto?' I ask her.

'Hamilton,' she says, 'but Clarissa, the girl he's marrying, comes from Toronto so that's where they're having the wedding.' She shows me a photograph of Liam who is a very handsome guy, and Clarissa, who is also very handsome, in a Tarzan sort of way.

'Now tell me,' Mrs McKenna says, 'does that look like a girl who'd want matching avocado dishes?'

To tell the truth, which I don't, Clarissa looks more as if she'd appreciate matching hockey sticks, or a Habitat punch bag, but now it's my turn, so I explain about Laura being a teacher and going on an exchange to Vancouver for a year and me going out to join her for the summer holiday on account of having enough dosh for the air fare. I won it.

'A competition?' says Mrs M, impressed.

'A Premium Bond,' I tell her, and she's even more impressed.

'I never met anyone who made money out of that racket before,' she says, 'though Patrick, my husband, won seventy-three and ninepence on the pools, back in '62. We splashed out. Had the fridge mended.'

'Isn't he going to the wedding?' I ask, really tactlessly. Why didn't I *think*? for she says, 'He's dead, dear. The Troubles.'

I think, Oh God, Belfast, and I wonder which side did it, and why, and that awful line they have on the News, shotbythesecurityforces, but before I can say anything else, Captain Bligh chips in again.

'Well, we're still on the tarmac,' he says, as if we hadn't noticed. 'Air traffic's very heavy over Northern Europe right now.'

Just like the M25. Then: '*Northern Europe*? We're going to Canada, aren't we?'

'Something to do with the way the earth spins, isn't it?' says Mrs M, vaguely. 'Still, I suppose *we're* Northern Europe really, aren't we?'

'And,' says Captain Bligh, who has not finished yet, by no means, 'we've had a little problem with a jammed fuel valve – '

'Jammed open or shut, I wonder,' murmurs Mrs McKenna, and I suddenly notice what a really dreadful smell of kerosene there is –

'– but that's all cleared up now and we have our fuel, so we *will* be leaving in a few minutes. Sorry for the slight delay, folks.'

Slight delay? An *hour*? 'He's very laid back, isn't he?' I say.

'Laid back? He's practically horizontal,' says Mrs McKenna. 'Isn't he the liar, though? Jammed valves, heavy traffic, increased security; what's he got to hide? I bet they're all asleep up there at the front – that happens, you know, on long-haul flights. The whole crew, snoring away, and the auto-pilot doing all the damage.'

I wonder if Mrs McKenna is going to come out with this sort of thing at regular intervals. Between her and Captain Bligh our flight should be a really restful experience.

Then suddenly – engines! Suddenly the terminal starts to slide away and the cabaret begins. Down the aisle come two air-hostesses – stewardesses – no, flight attendants they call them these days, what a come-down – hung about with demonstration seat-belts, oxygen masks and life-jackets, to show us what to do 'in the unlikely event of the plane coming down on water'. What's unlikely about that? I want to know. There's a lot of Atlantic between us and Canada.

'As opposed,' mutters Mrs McKenna, 'to the highly likely event of it disintegrating in mid-air, dear.' She *is* afraid. I know how she feels. If you keep talking about things that frighten you it's like a kind of insurance policy against them happening. Only flying doesn't make me feel like that. There is a voice-over and video with sign language, for the deaf, and the flight attendants mime to it, twirling the oxygen masks like they were doing a striptease. And you know that all the way up the aircraft this is going on, in every

63

cabin, synchronised safety drill. They must feel complete prats. Half a dozen fare-paying prats applaud.

'There's always some joker . . . ' says the stewardess on our aisle. I bet that's not in the script.

'They do that during taxiing,' says Mrs McKenna, 'so that we don't notice we're moving.' No flies on Mrs M.

And now the really fabulous bit, at the starting gate, revved up and straining to move on the end of the runway. Oh, this is when you can *feel* the power, about the only time on the whole flight when you understand why this damn great thing goes up and stays up. Once you're airborne you don't really have any sense of being . . . well, airborne; you might just as well be in a very noisy train, and turbulence feels like roller-skating over concrete.

Mrs McKenna is revved up to full twitch, too, eyes, fists and teeth clenched. She looks as if she is praying. 'Holy God, I could do with a fag,' she says.

And away we go.

Now comes the psychological bit; I really do believe that there is a psychologist involved here, somewhere, working out to the last second just how long you can leave airline passengers unoccupied before they go screaming mad with boredom or – like Mrs McKenna – fear. While Captain Bligh explains that we shall be flying at 33,000 feet, passing over Ireland, Greenland and Newfoundland on our way to Toronto (it still seems a cock-eyed way to me to get to Canada) the stewardesses clatter about behind bulkheads and hooray! here comes the drinks trolley, *all* the drinks trolleys; synchronised booze. Mrs McKenna, who lit

64

up as soon as the No Smoking signs went out, orders a large Scotch.

As soon as we are relaxing – well, as relaxed as some of us are ever going to get – with our drinks, it is lunchtime; or is it breakfast? This is where the clock begins to go haywire. Flying west the day goes on and on, getting longer and longer. When I get to Vancouver in fifteen hours' time it will still only be eight o'clock in the evening. Then, as soon as brunch has gone, it's the in-flight movie. I have noticed that there is always a lot of gratuitous violence in in-flight movies, perhaps to remind persons of a nervous disposition that things are a hell of a lot worse on the ground, but never much sex, to prevent us all from getting over-excited in a confined space. By now we have all been given our headsets hygienically sealed in polythene bags, but I *never* tune in to in-flight movies. I play this game with myself, pretending it's a silent film and seeing how much of the plot I can follow. Mrs McKenna has smoked herself to sleep; nervous exhaustion.

TransAt have discovered a brilliant way to make you feel that you are going nowhere slowly. They have this map on the video screen now that the movie has finished, showing the North Atlantic, and a little red aeroplane drawing a dotted line like a vapour trail, which is us, crawling across the ocean. Odd to think about what may be going on down there, because it's impossible to think of it as *down there*. I can never believe that I am 33,000 feet up. On the screen, at the bottom of the map, it says that we are 33,000 feet up, travelling at 651 miles an hour, but you can't feel it.

Six hundred and fifty-one miles an hour is pretty good going; perhaps we'll make up some of the time we lost at Heathrow. I wonder what the real reason was that we were so late taking off – I mean, if Captain Bligh hadn't made quite so many excuses – and if Mrs McKenna hadn't made that joke about carrying other people's presents . . .

Khalid.

They couldn't possibly have meant anyone like that, could they? The kind of people they are thinking of are strangers, surely, people who say, 'Look, so-and-so tells me you're going to Canada and I've got this cousin/sister/fiancée out there and parcel post costs the earth . . .'

That is more or less exactly what Khalid said.

'Look, Sandra,' he said, 'I'm not being mean or anything, but it would cost a fortune to post this lot, plus insurance.'

And what did I say? What *did* I say? 'But Laura's birthday isn't till October. I'll be gone by then.'

'Well, can't you get one of her friends to look after it? Or just give it to her and make her swear on pain of death not to open it until the day?'

Which is, of course, I suppose, why he taped it up so firmly. Just in case Laura will be tempted to look before she should.

Bulletproof, I said, didn't I? Bulletproof gift wrap. That paper is so thick you can't even feel that it is books inside. How do I know that it is books inside?

He *said* it is books. Books are rectangular. When I think of bombs I see something long and pointed, like a mortar shell, or round and black with BOMB written on the side. I do not think of a rectangle, not of anything shaped like a book. He said it was books. He even said which books; three volumes of some eighteenth-century essays, not quite first editions but with full calf bindings – and I *saw* them before he wrapped them up – because Laura loves old things. It's an odd sort of present to send to Canada, really; she'll only have to bring it all the way back when she comes home.

Of course it is books. He's not very practical, he'd never think about her having to lug them home, he was just so anxious for her to have them; he *was* anxious, wasn't he? He kept on and on at me to make sure I'd packed them safely, kept telling me not to carry them but to make sure they went in the hold because I'm quite likely to lose a flight bag; remember Swindon station – no, that was a suitcase – but I didn't see him actually wrapping them.

Anyway, postage to Canada isn't *that* expensive. Well, of course, it is, but not to him, not compared with what he must have spent on the books – even the wrapping paper looks like Harrods. I said that, didn't I?

The little plane on the map must be stuck. We've been hovering just off Greenland for hours, I'll swear we have. Why would Khalid want to blow up an airliner? He's an Arab. I'm not even sure where he comes from, Dubai, Bahrain, somewhere quiet, not like Gaza or Beirut, and I don't even notice him being an Arab now. I couldn't help it at first, because we don't know any Arabs apart from him, but he has hardly any accent and doesn't wear one of those Yasser Arafat tea-towels. He's studying company law, to be an accountant, and he means to stay in England, he says; he's going to buy a house, he's going to stay in England and marry Laura, if Laura hasn't changed her mind and run off with a lumber baron. That was Mum's joke, not mine. He's going to stay in England and marry Laura and I shall be his sister-in-law.

We are over Greenland at last. How long have we got to go? I'm not even sure what time it is. I forgot to reset my watch, and the little red plane crawls on.

Khalid would never have given *me* a bomb to carry for him. He likes me. He loves Laura, he wouldn't do that to us. Terrorists would do it to anyone, that is how they operate; no one is safe; everyone is a legitimate target. That's what they say in Northern Ireland, isn't it? If the IRA want to kill someone they call him a legitimate target. Anyone can be a legitimate target, not just the soldier but the soldier's wife, the soldier's child . . . You can't call yourself an innocent bystander any more. If a terrorist decides to kill you, you deserve to die.

There must be nearly 500 people on this plane. If Khalid has . . .

I can't even think it. How could I say it?

When they asked me if I was carrying a letter or a package for anyone else I never thought of Khalid. They couldn't have made it any plainer, but I didn't think.

If Khalid has given me . . .

If it isn't books . . .

You can't tell what it is. They use cassette players these days, don't they? Semtex, that can't be detected, detonated by barometric pressure.

We're at 33,000 feet. What height is it meant to

go off at? Thirty-three thousand feet isn't all that high. I've flown at 36,000 just going up to Scotland.

If Khalid has caused me to bring a bomb on board I shall be responsible for killing 500 people. And me.

It could go off at any second.

I might never even finish thinking this.

I shall have to tell somebody.

It could go off even as I put out my finger to press the buzzer for the stewardess.

If I tell anyone, what good would it do? You can't get into the hold from the cabins. Would we turn back? We must be past the point of no return, by now. No return, ever.

It can't be true. I'm just imagining it. I am not the sort of person who . . .

Laura is a pessimist; she says, 'Anything that *can* happen can happen to *you*.' I always think, It can't happen to me. Anyone who flies has to think that. It can't happen to me because nothing ever does happen to me. I don't know how many times I have flown, but nothing ever happens except delays. When the car crashed on the autostrada I wasn't even bruised, and everybody else had fractures and whiplash.

Here's the stewardess now. My mouth is so dry, what can I say to her? Excuse me, I think we may have a bomb on board.

'Yes?' she says, switching out my light.

'May I have some mineral water, please? With ice?'

Because I still don't believe it. I don't think I even meant to press that button.

Or is it predestination? I meant to press it, but something – someone – *didn't* mean me to; so I didn't say what I . . .

69

Some people believe in a Plan. Everything that happens has been planned in advance, and all the things that ever happened before, contributed to it. Like, if this plane is destined to blow up, 500 people have been doomed to die on the flight TA002 because I am on it. I cannot prevent it. I am on flight TA002 because I won fifteen hundred pounds on the Premium Bonds. I have the Premium Bond because my gran bought it for me as a christening present seventeen years ago – no, sixteen years and eleven months ago. Ernie was predestined to choose my number, which is mine because Gran was predestined to be in the Post Office at a certain moment on a certain morning in a certain place in the queue. Laura was predestined to meet Khalid in Paris on March 23rd, 1988 because she happened to go into the Pompidou Centre at a certain moment. Nothing has ever happened to me because I have been saved for this one thing – to carry the bomb.

It is nonsense. There is no bomb.

The stewardess is coming back with my mineral water. I shall tell her now.

'Coffee, dear, and a large Scotch.' I didn't notice Mrs McKenna waking up. Mr McKenna died in the Troubles – but not Mrs McKenna. Her number had not come up. Is it coming up now?

If I did tell them, what could they do? Come down in the Atlantic? No, what *could* they do?

The stewardess comes back with Mrs McKenna's coffee and Scotch and the little red aeroplane crawls on down over Greenland, going south at last, down towards Newfoundland, and we go on and we go on at 663 miles an hour, 665, 672, at 33,000 feet, and we go on and we are still here. And I wonder, when it happens, do you know?

It's only because Khalid is an Arab. If he was English or French or German and he'd given me that parcel, would I be thinking what I am thinking now?

What's this? Tea? Lunch? 'No, no, thank you. Just coffee.'

The map: 28,000 feet; are we coming down? Of course we are; beginning our descent to Toronto. If it was a barometric detonator it didn't work, or didn't we ever get high enough? Thirty-three thousand feet isn't all that high, and nothing happened going up so nothing will happen coming down. And when we get to Toronto we change on to the Vancouver flight and the hold will be opened and the baggage will be transferred and I can tell someone.

'Good afternoon,' says Captain Bligh. It *is* still afternoon. Has he been asleep while we crossed the Atlantic? Have I been asleep? Have I dreamed it all? *I woke up. It was all a dream.*

I haven't been asleep. I feel as if I had, that muddled, dry-mouth feeling, but I haven't slept. It isn't a dream.

'Did you hear that?' says Mrs McKenna.

'No, what?'

'They're bringing round Customs declarations, dear, for foreigners. That's us.'

A white card drops into my lap. A lot of questions about any prohibited goods I might be carrying. They seem mainly worried about seeds.

'We'll be landing in thirty minutes,' says Captain Bligh.

Perhaps he's telling the truth, for once.

'I think we'll be parting company, here,' says
Mrs McKenna. 'Aren't you going on to Vancouver?'

What happens to the luggage here? I have to
find out for certain because this time I really must
do something before those suitcases are put on the
Vancouver flight. I must warn someone, whatever
they say – and whatever will Laura say – I mean, what
will they do? Put my suitcases out on the tarmac and
destroy them with a controlled explosion? I couldn'
hide what had happened from Laura. She'll find out
Khalid will find out, he'll know that I believed that
he was capable of – and I shall never know if he did
or he didn't.

I sign my form. 'What do we do with this?'

'Hand it in at Passport Control,' says a passing
flight attendant.

'Excuse me – '

He doesn't hear. He was predestined not to hear.

We're down. I haven't even noticed that we are
landing. We're in Lester B Pearson International Air
port, but by the view from the window it might jus
as well be Heathrow. Perhaps I *have* been asleep.
could have dreamed the whole flight. Perhaps we ar
still at Heathrow and any moment Captain Bligh wi
come on the air with another lie about delays.

But people are getting up and opening luggag
bins. Another voice, not Captain Bligh, tells everyon
to remain seated and belted up until we stop taxiin
but no one takes any notice, so I fetch down my stuf
and Mrs McKenna's.

'Trouble with us people with filthy habits,' says M
McKenna, 'stuck up here in the tail, we're always th

72

last off, last in the queue through Immigration.' And she's right.

Oh God, the waiting. Why don't they open the doors? This bit I always hate, it's the same in any queue that doesn't move, even at a cash till, that *constipated* feeling.

'I don't smoke,' I say, but too late. The queue surges. Mrs McKenna, being small and sharp, bores away like a woodworm and that's the last I see of her.

Out of the window I notice baggage handlers at the forward hold.

'Goodbye,' says the flight attendant at the door and I am out of the plane, almost running down the tunnel that bounces slightly; think of being trapped in here with flames advancing; follow the signs with suitcases on, but no suitcases for me; Immigration; passports.

End of the queue again, just like Mrs McKenna said, but a bit of luck at last, there were more Canadians than foreigners on that flight, we're going through fast, so fast that I only wish we weren't. Because in a minute I've got to make up my mind what to do, and decide; do I tell the Immigration Officer, or whoever he is – ?

'And what is the purpose of your visit?'

'A holiday. I'm visiting my sister in Vancouver.'

'On which date do you intend to leave Canada?'

'August 30th.'

Smack. He stamps the passport.

And now: 'Through to the left,' he says, 'and collect your baggage.'

'My baggage?'

'Haven't you got any baggage?' He smiles.

'But I'm going on to Vancouver.'

'Yes, but you go through Customs *here*,' he says.

Am I floating away from him . . . into the baggage hall . . . to the carousel? Look for the sign, Flight TA002.

I can get it back.

Will it be one of those times when mine is last, when I stand there getting more and more certain that it will never appear? I see my rainbow luggage strap. I see three, none of them mine, oh God, the things people take on aircraft, great lumping boxes, parcels, trunks, polystyrene cartons big enough to ship a grand piano, round they rumble. Where's mine? Have they found something out there behind the curtains? It's like a crematorium, you can imagine a coffin on there, going round and round.

There, *there*! No, you fool, that's mine. It isn't. It *is*. It is, and it's standing on one end; down it goes, *splat*. Oh, come on; it's not going to go off now, after all it's been through. Where's the other one – *there*.

Maybe it wasn't a barometric detonator, maybe it's a timing device. We're an hour and a half late. If it was a time bomb it ought to have gone off by now –

It's another five hours to Vancouver.

And at last it's in my hands again. I am carrying it. I can't remember which suitcase it was in, but I've got it back. A trolley, a trolley, where – ?

It's so heavy. Books are heavy. Real books are. I remember when he gave them to me; bombs don't weigh as much as books. That's why he didn't want to post them, because of the weight.

The Customs hall is right ahead, but no one's

74

being stopped. Don't they care what we bring into the country? Perhaps they know who to look for.

Mum says it's not worth locking suitcases, your experienced thief just slashes. So all I have to do now is unbuckle the strap and take it out – no, wrong case – take it out in its Harrods wrapping and carry it through.

Carry it?

I'm holding it. It *is* books, I can feel it is, put it in the flight bag and open it in the loo or something. Wait, get rid of the cases first, send them on to Vancouver. I may never join them there, why doesn't someone come over and demand to know why I am fiddling suspiciously with my luggage.

And away they go, my suitcases, my harmless cases full of clothes.

Into the Ladies where no one can see me.

Feel it again. I've been kidding myself, it could be anything in there. If it is books, where are the corners, the curves of the spines?

Khalid, I do believe you, I do trust you, but I have to look.

The tape tears the pattern from the paper when I lift it, but it comes away. Underneath, cardboard, layers of cardboard; of course, to protect the bindings. That's why I couldn't feel any corners. He's made up a sort of box from cornflakes packets. Honestly, he can be so mean about some things. After spending a fortune on books, too mean to buy a jiffy-bag, too mean to post them. But he may have been afraid the bindings would get damaged.

It is books: beautiful white leather, a gold coat of arms stamped on the covers, gilded pages.

75

He could have hollowed them out. You see that in old films, books that are only shells, containing guns, contraband.

No, just pages. Just paper. Just books. Khalid is only Khalid, not a terrorist, not a multiple murderer. I knew that all the time, didn't I? I *knew*, I was sure; if I hadn't been sure I'd never have opened the parcel in here and risked blowing up Lester B Pearson International Airport.

I have been a bloody fool, right through. Being certain of Khalid wasn't enough, I could have killed hundreds of people, here, in the plane, at Heathrow, even. That's what terrorists do, they terrify you. They make you suspect everyone, they make you suspect yourself.

I seal up the parcel again. Laura will be able to tell that it's been opened but I can always pretend that they made me do it at Customs. I shall never be able to see Khalid again without thinking of this, without remembering what I thought he could do, without remembering what I did, and what I didn't do.

If we hadn't been delayed we'd have had three hours here in Toronto, but already they're calling the flight to Vancouver, and I must go out of here and get on that plane knowing that I am innocent, and Khalid is innocent, and there is nothing worse than books in my flight bag and clothes in my suitcases. I was right to trust him. I stand at the departure gate and look at the other passengers, and wonder who they have trusted.

LOCAL KNOWLEDGE

Margaret Mahy

As Simpson was sliding back into place beside
Harrington, something, perhaps the movement of
a night animal, made him turn quickly. His elbow
accidentally struck the wall beside him which gave
out a curious echoing boom. It was not very loud
and yet it seemed to make the whole night ring in
sympathy.

In the darkness the wall had certainly appeared
to be solid stone, overgrown with creeping rosemary
and other wandering scented herbs. Now, as its cry
rang through in the air around him, he understood
that he had struck a water-tank, possibly alerting the
man inside the house, whoever he might happen to
be. In those circumstances, it sounded like a sudden
announcement, although the night around them was
not particularly silent. In fact it was active . . . even
alarmed. Earlier they had been startled by possums
running along the top of the wall and snickering
down at them. Then some small unidentified animal
had screamed aloud, probably for good reason. All
the time in a cabin of its own in a gully on the
other side of the house, a generator throbbed like

77

an angry heart. Nevertheless, Simpson waited for some response to the booming water-tank . . . for quick footsteps or slamming doors.

As it happened nothing in the house recognised the tank's alarmed cry. There was no alteration in the diffuse glow on the camellias and birches to the left of the house where light spread sideways from a kitchen window. The fragmented shadow of the man inside did not, as far as they could tell from its broken outline, stiffen or turn in any way.

'God!' muttered Harrington, after the first frozen moment had gone by. 'Wake the whole place up, why don't you?'

'Sorry, mate,' Simpson muttered back, rubbing his arm, becoming aware, as his first concentration relaxed, that it was numb from shoulder to wrist. 'It's so bloody overgrown around here. Hey, he's at the kitchen sink . . . whichever one of them he is.'

'Did you get a good look at him?'

'Not very! The ground falls away there,' Simpson said, 'and anyhow everything is so bloody dry he'd have heard me crackling around in the undergrowth if I'd tried to get closer.' He hesitated. 'I got the impression of curly hair. Jerry Macmillan had his clipped short, didn't he?'

In the darkness Harrington looked first disappointed, then mulish.

'Suppose it's the other one, Jacko, in there; he just might have decided to hide his dear twin brother Jerry from the law, mightn't he? No matter what the brother had done?'

'I reckon Jerry'll make for the airport,' Simpson said. 'He's mad if he doesn't!'

'They say he *is* mad,' Harrington replied. 'But anyhow that's someone else's problem. Our job is to check him out here. Very tactfully!' He paused. 'I'm not coming over all intuitive or anything like that,' he added, 'but I just have a feeling about this place . . . '

And he glanced about the shadowed shifting garden, felt the day's heat reflecting up into the night around him, then up at the stars, unexpectedly bright and clear to a man used to the ambient light of the city. Orion hung head downwards, curving back towards the east, a sprawling summer clown rather than a hero.

'So let's go,' Simpson said. 'Everything's in place.' Harrington paused, checking things over in his mind.

Into his pause came a new sound, soft and definite, seeming at first to come from several different directions at once. Harrington and Simpson shrank back, peering along the narrow path that ran below the high wall with the water-tank built into it. The path, covered as it was in small white shells, glimmered eerily, and Harrington suddenly realised that what they were hearing was shells crunching under shoes. Suddenly a dark shape appeared in the darkness on the edge of the verandah, moved swiftly across it, and opened the door much more confidently than a casual visitor. She had come boldly around a path at the side of the house, walking without hesitation though she had no torch. A diffuse light coming from inside showed them the shape of a head . . . flowing hair . . . the rippled edge of a skirt and the straight line of the stick she carried . . . not the usual white stick, Harrington remembered, realising who it must be, but an elegant wooden one with a heavily maned lion's head on it. He had seen it at her own house, the only other house on the headland, when he was checking things out a little earlier.

For a moment they saw her poised there in the doorway, saw her turn her head and look back down the path as if she knew they were there watching her. Then she stepped inside, closing the door firmly after her. The shadow on the camellias moved sharply, sliding across the lighted patch and vanishing. Someone in the house was moving rapidly across the room to intercept the visitor.

'God, that was quick,' Simpson said. 'Who on earth . . . ?'

'Elizabeth Garland from the other house,' Harrington said, nodding angrily in the direction she had come from though there were no lights to be seen. 'What does she think she's doing? How did she get up here without the others seeing her? Local knowledge I suppose.'

'What?' said Simpson.

'I saw her about twenty minutes ago, and she offered to call in and check things out for me. She said she might be able to tell if Jacko Macmillan was on his own or if he had Jerry hidden away in the wardrobe or whatever! She said she had local knowledge.'

'Is that what she's up to or do you reckon she's just popped over to borrow a cup of sugar?' Simpson asked.

'No,' said Harrington bitterly. 'I reckon she's trying to be clever. But we'll wait a moment and see what happens. If Jerry's in there we don't want to alarm him and wind up with some sort of hostage drama on our hands.'

'Better be ready to move in *fast* though,' Simpson added.

'Very fast,' agreed Harrington grimly.

Opening the door from the entrance hall Liz sensed someone immediately on the other side of it waiting for her, and said his name aloud, rather forcefully, as if by naming him she might compel the invisible man into a familiar form.

'Jacko!'

'Liz?' asked an astonished but totally familiar voice.

'Who did you think it was?' she asked him, hearing her own voice, cool and amused in the warm night. 'Don't sound so surprised. It's not that late.'

'It feels like midnight,' the man answered, still sounding bewildered. 'I've been working. I'm only just getting dinner ready. Are you passing by, or paying a proper visit?'

He put his arm around her as he spoke.

'A bit of both,' she said. 'It's a passing visit.' She turned inwards towards him, hugged him and then stepped away into a room looking through a wide expanse of window across a harbour which at this time of night was a murmuring darkness. Not entirely dark however. Far over to the left radiant patches would be marking the city port. On the opposite side of the harbour another sprinkle of lights would be outlining a residential area connected to the port by a ferry service, but in between these stippled islands lay in a loop of darkness, Liz's own territory, though not because she lived in darkness

81

in quite the way people supposed. They found it hard to believe that her eyes which could not see the world could still see moving colours, a frequent marbling of blue and green. Most people thought of her blindness as unyielding blackness. Liz, who had felt her way around this room over and over again, just as she had felt her way over all the tracks and hidden paths on the headland from childhood on, knew exactly where the window was, and looked out of it, inventing her own image of what was there, an image built up of words, of the patient descriptions that Jacko had given her. She knew this house as well as she knew her own, as well as she knew the tracks that wound the two houses together.

'Drink?' Jacko asked cheerfully from behind her.

'Thanks,' said Liz. 'But let me get it myself.' She walked across the room towards the kitchen cupboard. The one room contained kitchen and living space. The seaside cabin it had once been had been added to over the years. Lamps and candles had given way to electric power and the clunk of the generator. As she moved, Jacko stepped out of her way, but then moved up very silently behind her, standing only inches away as she put up her hand to a shelf. In the light his curling hair shone as if it were wet or alive with metallic threads. This and his wide smile made him seem almost like a mechanical man, or an android, almost but not quite human. There was no one in the room to notice this however.

Liz failed to find what she had expected to find, paused, running her long hands lightly over the stainless steel around the sink.

She felt vegetables under her fingers, potatoes

and carrots, felt the grains of dirt still clinging to their skins. She touched them, picked up one of the potatoes, ran her fingers over its uneven surface. 'You're cooking a whole meal,' she exclaimed.

He stepped back from her so that his words would not be spoken immediately into her ear. 'I'm starving,' he said. His voice sounded gentle and plaintive, but the grin that accompanied them was savage. 'Man must eat!'

'Well, you've shifted the bottle,' she said in a resigned voice. 'Perhaps you'd better pour me a drink after all.'

But he was already pouring red wine. His eyes glinted and seemed to move a little as they reflected the heavy crimson flow. He was a tall strong man, a wide forehead and sleepy eyelids below his glistening curls. He put the glass into her hand.

'Thanks,' she said. 'But don't let me interrupt you,' she added, nodding towards the vegetables and the kitchen sink.

Jacko hesitated. 'Did you come here for any special reason?' he asked her. 'Or just to be nice?'

'I came for all sorts of reasons,' she said, 'but not the sort of reasons that need to interrupt dinner.'

Jacko nodded. 'I'm starving,' he said again. She was looking more or less in his direction. Abruptly he pulled a hideous face at her, then stared back intently at her, almost as if he expected some reaction, but as she continued to smile placidly a little to his left, he relaxed, and smiled to himself in a pleased way before moving back to the kitchen and waiting vegetables.

'Did you know Jerry has escaped?' she asked him suddenly in her cool disinterested voice.

'Of course,' he answered. 'I think I knew the very hour and minute. I almost felt it in myself. Twins do that sometimes. How did you know?'

'It was on the news with warnings,' she said. 'And as you haven't got television or radio, I thought you mightn't know. I'd forgotten about the mystic twinly bond.'

'Oh well, it wasn't just that. I had a call from the police earlier in the day,' he said. 'They naturally imagined he might look for me. I explained that we hadn't seen anything of one another for years. Literally years. I mean on our last day together he tried to kill *me*, didn't he? Talk about self-destruction! I've kept out of his way since then.'

'You write to him though,' she said.

'That!' he said bitterly, and fell silent, turning on the tap so that the room was filled with the sound of flowing water.

'They say he killed someone as he escaped,' said Liz restlessly. 'It's hard to believe that any relation of yours could beat someone's head in.' She moved across in front of the window and sat down on the end of the window-seat beside a small table which held a bowl full of polished stones and a small lamp, dark under its parchment shade. 'Why is he *like* that?'

Jacko turned back from the sink, his hand on the tap. 'Jerry was always mad and bad and dangerous to know,' he said lightly. 'He was dashing . . . wild . . . rebellious . . . '

'Yes, but he never quite *sounds* like that,' Liz said. 'I mean, I know he was supposed to be the adventurous one, but it all seems to me like just another way of saying he was a spoiled boy who wanted everything to go *his* way.'

She put her glass down on the edge of the table. Jacko, standing by the sink with the water flowing down over his hands, stared into the twisted transported column, moving yet still, as if it might suddenly reveal magical images.

'You've never even met him,' he said sharply. 'Jerry's remarkable in his way, and somehow life has never quite treated him fairly . . . never *acknowledged* him . . . not really. Oh well, he'll give them a run for their money.' And then he straightened and laughed, sliding the potato peeler skilfully over the potato.

'What would you do if he *did* come here?' she asked.

'Oh, don't you worry,' he said bitterly. 'I'd certainly refuse to help him if that's what you're worrying about. I'd tell him to turn himself in. I'd tell him he should get help of some kind. If he wouldn't agree to that I'd give him twenty minutes to get clear and ring the cops. Well, twenty-five minutes maybe, for old time's sake. That's exactly what I'd do. Dr Jekyll always tries to distance himself from Mr Hyde. Never mind!' He turned towards her, lifting his glass in his left hand, water dripping from his fingers. 'Cheers!'

'Here's to rainy days!' said Liz, lifting hers.

He gave her a quizzical look, putting his glass down to take up another potato.

'It's just as well he doesn't know how great things are for us,' she said. 'He sounds like the sort of man who would feel lessened by anyone else's good luck or happiness.'

'I suppose so,' Jacko replied in a noncommital voice.

'Or by anything that he wasn't in charge of,' Liz repeated. 'Especially anything happening to *you*, because apparently you're so like him, but somehow more in *charge* than he could ever be. Mr Hyde always had to envy Dr Jekyll. I can't help feeling sorry for your Jerry.'

'Sorry!' exclaimed Jacko. He looked furious. 'A man with his record . . . half the police in the country watching ports and airports . . . how can you be *sorry* for him? He's dangerous. If he came this way, his head would be echoing with the sound of bones giving way. Once you've heard that I'll bet you go on hearing it. Sorry indeed!'

'I just am,' she answered calmly. 'I'm sorry for anyone who has to work so hard to get a starring role. But don't let's talk about him any more.' She shivered. 'It's as if his ghost were in the room with us, making me cold.'

Jacko turned away from the kitchen sink to the stove putting potatoes into a saucepan and a steamer. The only sound was the watery flow of the tap and, beyond the walls, out in the night, the distant chug of the generator.

Liz shivered again. 'I'll put the heater on,' she said.

'If you like,' he said. 'It seems hot to me, but perhaps it's just the memory of the day.'

She went unerringly to a little cupboard, brought out a two-bar heater which she plugged in, next to the plug belonging to the lamp, and switched it on. She shifted her chair so that she sat before it, warming her hands. Her stick leaned against the table.

'It's been a scorcher of a day but it's a beautiful night,' she said dreamily. 'I could feel it all around me as I walked up the hill.' But he did not reply, simply scraped the last carrots under the soft flow of the tap. She got to her feet restlessly and crossed the room.

'Where are you going?' he asked sharply.

She laughed. 'Just a call of nature, for goodness sake!'

'Don't go into the bedroom!' he said uneasily. 'I've got work spread about all over the floor.'

'That's a change for you . . . telling me to stay out of the bedroom I mean,' she said. 'You're usually trying to lure me there.'

'But not when the floor's covered with paper,' he replied in a mechanical way.

As soon as she had left the room he leaped across to the door which was not properly closed, watching her confident progress down the short passage and through a door to the right. Then he seemed to relax, wandered back to the sink, turned the tap off, put the carrots into a steamer and on to the stove. But all the time he was listening, anxious to hear the door in the passage open and close, to hear the bathroom door next to it open, and the brief rush of water as she washed her hands, the pause while she dried them, her footsteps coming back into the room. As she came out again, smiling, he was waiting for her, catching her arm and bending his head to stare curiously into her unfocused eyes. Then very slowly he kissed her mouth. She put her arms around his neck and pressed herself against him, but almost as if she was trying to avoid him, by forcing herself so close to

87

him there would not be enough space between them for him to touch her or kiss her again. Nevertheless, as her face, slightly averted, was looking over his shoulder, he kissed her ear and the side of her neck, and at this third kiss she shuddered uncontrollably. He released her immediately, stepping back, smiling his earlier savage smile.

'It's funny, that!' he said as she moved past him wordlessly, obstinately seeking her chair by the lamp that lit nothing, and the glowing heater. 'You'd think lips would be truest of all.'

'What do you mean?' she asked, but now her composure was cracking. Her voice shook a little.

'The neck,' he said. 'It always seems like the bit that joins the head to the body, an in-between piece, charming in its own way, of course, but not like the heart, or eyes or mouth, not like a touchstone, a thing that might tell the truth.' He moved back to the stove, tilted the lid of the saucepan and looked in at the vegetables. Then he turned to face her once more, though she was not facing him.

'I've always rather liked necks,' he said, and then without a pause, 'You *know*, don't you? Your neck gave you away. It positively *crept*!'

Liz looked a little past him. 'Yes, of course I do. I thought so immediately, and when I heard you peeling potatoes I was sure. Where's Jacko? In the bedroom?' she asked.

'Spread out on the floor with his throat cut from ear to ear,' replied Jerry, smiling widely.

'That's nonsense,' she said. 'It would be too much like killing yourself. Where *is* he?'

'What does it matter? I'm here; we're identical, you know.'

'Only to the rest of the world, not to one another,' she said. 'And not to me! I'm not misled by false clues like appearance.'

Jerry had picked up the knife from the bench.

'He used to write to me, not about anything much,' he said, touching the point over and over again. A bead of blood appeared on his forefinger. 'I had to read between the lines,' he went on, watching the drop of blood swell and trickle. Then he pulled off the wig of glistening curls and casually hung it on a cup hook. 'Look!' he said, 'I'm not him. Look at *me*!' and then added irritably, 'I keep forgetting that you can't. He wrote about you, this incredible blind woman. Everything he had was partly mine . . . even you.'

'I belong to myself,' she said. 'I want to know about Jacko. That's why I came.'

'Let me tell you about myself,' he suggested. 'Imagine someone exactly the same as Jacko but much brighter. Right this moment I'm coming towards you, and I'm holding a *knife*,' he told her. 'It's about a foot long with a black handle and a thin blade. It's newly sharpened.' He ran his thumb very tenderly, very lightly across the blade. 'Hear that?'

Liz let her hand fall down beside her chair. She found a switch and turned it on. For a moment, the light on the table flowered white and strong under its parchment hood, then the whole room, the whole house, was plunged into darkness. Jerry swore, flinging out his hand before him, and, hearing her leap to her feet, moved himself, clumsily making for the door, so that she would not escape, but as he moved there was the sound of shattering glass. The lights of the harbour seemed to him to shatter too. Stars seemed to rush in on him.

'Wait till I get you,' he said, furiously stabbing at the dark, but the sound of the breaking glass had been also the breaking of a spell. He heard the front door bursting open, and at the same moment something struck him with such power, such fury that he experienced not just pain but a great burst of white light, much more explosive than the light of the table lamp had been, light exploding from somewhere inside his head. As he fell to his knees, other lights, the beams of powerful torches transfixed him. There were men there, ready to seize him, to disarm him, to thrust him against the wall and twist his arm behind his back, but there was no need. Blinded by pain and by the light inside his head, he toppled into incoherence, feeling, just as if it had been branded upon him, the imprint, the very fangs, of the roaring lion.

'I had to know about Jacko!' Liz said. Though she was still shaking, her earlier composure persistently haunted her voice and gestures. 'How is he now?' The words were simple but they came out strangely. She was frightened of what the answer might be.

'Really, he'll be fine in a day or two,' Simpson said. 'That precious brother of his must have given him quite a bang. He's been badly concussed but . . . he's got a hard head.'

'Mind you,' said Harrington, 'you certainly gave Jerry a dose of his own medicine.'

'Jerry said he'd killed him,' Liz said and suddenly

tears ran down her face and dripped from her chin into her cup of tea.

'He exaggerated,' said Simpson. 'My God, they certainly did look alike. He must have got that wig in a joke shop. It wouldn't have fooled anyone close up.'

Tears continued to flow down Liz's face, but under them she smiled a little. 'I'm not distracted by appearance,' she said. 'I can't be, can I? When I first came he hugged me and I could smell something different, something like new nylon or whatever. I didn't think of a wig.'

'When were you sure?' Harrington asked.

'I was completely sure when I heard him scraping the potatoes with the tap running. I knew it must be Jerry then. Jacko would never do that . . . not at this time of year.'

'This time of year?' Harrington asked, glancing over at her in surprise.

'Not in summer,' she said, sounding surprised. 'There's not enough water. You could hear it yourself.'

Simpson and Harrington looked at one another uncertainly, and sensing their doubt, she laughed, wiping her tears away with the back of her hand. 'You must have heard the sound the tank gave off when you banged it. I heard it as I was coming up the hill. I thought it must be you or someone like you. Possums make a different sound.'

Simpson gave a silly grin.

'Tanks only boom like that if they're empty,' she went on. 'Local knowledge! A full tank gives a funny dead thudding sound. And Jacko would never let the

91

water run away. He'd run it into that red plastic bowl in the cupboard under the sink, wash the vegetables in it and then pour it out over the camellias. I sat there, hearing the water flowing as if it didn't matter so I knew it must be Jerry.'

'Weren't you frightened?' asked Simpson.

'I was terrified,' she said. 'But I had heard you outside, so I knew there was somebody I could call on. I hoped that something like a window breaking would bring you in.'

'Lucky for you there was a blackout, though,' Simpson said.

Harrington gave him an exasperated look. 'Tell him!' he said to Liz.

'The power supply always cuts out if there's an overload,' she explained, smiling and shivering as she spoke. 'I knew exactly how much power it would take. Three lights, the stove and the heater! Well, the kitchen light had to be on . . . he was working there . . . I knew the lamp was *off* because when it's on I can feel it warm on my neck. I turned the heater on and later when I went to the lavatory I turned the bathroom light on and left it going. All I had to do was to switch the lamp on to overload everything, and make it cut out, and *then* listen carefully to the way he moved. I wasn't in any real danger.'

'Anything could have gone wrong,' said Harrington.

'I promise never to do it again!' she said. 'May I see my poor old boyfriend now?'

'I sent for the ambulance but for the present he's in his own bed,' said Simpson, getting up to help her.

'I know the way,' she told him, and left the room, eager and unaided.

THE MAN IN THE LIFT

Rex Harley

On the desk in front of me is a pile of essays that I've stopped marking. The reason is the piece of work on top: the one I've just read. Of course, there may be nothing to worry about. I know well enough that the author has a wilder imagination than most.

Ronald Jefferies. If I had to fill in one of those character reference forms for him, I'd probably start with 'gifted but odd' or 'odd but gifted'; it depends which angle you view him from. And as for his latest offering – do I put a mark on the end of it, together with an appropriately ironic comment, or do I admit that it troubles me and I don't know what to do about it?

One more time. I'll read it once more, and then I shall be certain.

"I'm in my bedroom. The door's closed, which means I'm supposed to be doing my homework. Somewhere downstairs Mum and Dad are watching television, and Karen's gone to the youth club with her friends. I remember when I was thirteen playing ping-pong seemed vaguely exciting, a sort of escape, so I don't take the mickey out of her.

I should be writing a timed essay for English which is why I've got the alarm-clock next to me. I bought it at a jumble sale, from the White Elephant stall. It's chrome-plated and I shined it up when I got home. 'American Alarms. Patent Pending. 1908' it says on the back. It's got this amazingly frantic bell too. But I don't use it as an alarm-clock. The tick's too loud. Keeps me awake half the night, and at the moment I seem to do that well enough without any assistance.

Why? Because I think I'm in trouble; and that's something I normally manage to steer clear of: I keep my eyes and ears open, I can run quite fast and, if the worst comes to the worst, I do a pretty good line in grovelling. Say the Fifth Year thugs corner you behind the dustbins. If you say the right things and hand over enough money for them to buy another pack of Marlboro, they generally give you a reprieve. So long as you don't try to sound too smart. 'Actually' is a word to avoid. I've only used it the once. 'Where do you think you're going, Jefferies?' 'Well, actually— ' I didn't even manage to finish the sentence before I was grabbed. Still, you learn from your mistakes. Now, I'd never antagonise a neanderthal with vocabulary.

But those characters never gave me sleepless nights. It was the trip to the Barbican that did it; the school trip to *Macbeth*.

> Methought I heard a voice cry 'Sleep no more!
> Macbeth does murder sleep.'

Ironic that.

The play itself was great. Dark. Claustrophobic. Everything closing in on Macbeth, even the scenery, so that by the end it's as if he's physically trapped in a little box.

The only problem was that they played the whole thing without an interval, so as soon as the applause had died down, everyone flooded out and into the toilets. My seat was bang in the middle of the circle so I was one of the last out, and by the time I'd finished, the rest of my party had disappeared.

That left me with a dilemma: either I waited where I was until someone realised I was missing; or I tried to find my way back to the coach alone. The trouble is that I have no sense of direction at all, and the Barbican is built like a multi-dimensional maze. You're supposed to work out where you're going by following a yellow line painted on the ground, like Theseus and his ball of string! This takes you up steps, down steps, along walkways, past doors into tower-block flats, round a floodlit church that's presumably there only because someone wouldn't let them knock it down, and, if you're very lucky, out into the streets of London. I didn't much fancy my chances of making it, to be honest, but it seemed so feeble just to stand there and wait that I left the theatre and set off along the nearest walkway.

For a while I even felt I knew where I was going, but the feeling didn't last long. I'd hoped to keep my bearings by the church in the centre of the whole complex, but soon even that had vanished and I found myself bumbling round walkways I'd not seen on the way *into* the theatre, and on completely the wrong level. I checked my watch by one of the yellowish lights at the entrance to a block of flats. Fifteen minutes since the performance ended. The others would be sitting on the coach and cries of 'Where the hell's Jefferies got to? Bloody typical!' would be starting up. Meantime, here I was scooting round the Barbican like a headless chicken.

At this point I decided it might be sensible to go back to the theatre and hang around until some irate teacher came to find me – and sod the humiliation. Then I realised I no longer knew where the theatre was either. The only solution was to step into the nearest block of flats and ask someone for directions; certainly there was no one around on that God-forsaken walkway.

I must admit that the idea of ringing a doorbell and bursting unknown and unannounced into somebody's evening made me a bit anxious: for some reason I expect strangers to be hostile. So for a moment or two I stood in the entrance hall, dithering near the lift. Just then I heard its winding gear grind into action. The lights above the lift doors showed that it was coming down from several floors above. As I hadn't called it there was presumably a passenger, which solved my problem quite neatly. I could ask *them*.

I watched the light go out as the lift moved between floors, then on, then off again, and still it was heading down to my level. At last I could hear it slowing to a standstill then, as the bell pinged to announce the opening of the doors, a thought struck me. Whoever was about to leave the lift had no idea I was there. If I advanced on them with an 'Excuse me but . . . ' what would they think? Probably that I was a drunk or a mugger. Maybe I should stand well clear and let them get out into the open.

As I was debating all this the doors opened and I found myself staring, not into a surprised face, but at the back wall of the lift. Nobody there at all. Then I looked down towards the floor.

Sitting in the corner with his legs stuck straight out in front of him, was a man. Mid forties. Foreign, I thought. His head was tipped forward on to his chest so I couldn't see his face. His hair was black and wiry, greying at the sides. He was breathing erratically. So much for my worrying about being taken for a drunk. The drunk was in the lift and spark out for the night! Better leave him where he was and try the next block of flats.

Just then his eyes flicked open and he stared straight at me. Very slowly his hand came up off the floor and he beckoned. I was rooted to the spot.

Then he mumbled something. I couldn't hear what it was so I stepped into the lift; it rocked slightly on its winding cable. The expression on the man's face was horrible. It was like a mixture of pain and pleading. And he was still holding out his hand towards me. In it I could suddenly make out the edge of a piece of paper. Without thinking what I was doing, I reached down to take it from him. He nodded as if to encourage me, and the pain on his face seemed to double.

As I pulled the paper from his grip I heard the thud of the door mechanism. I was about to be trapped in the lift with him. I panicked, whirled round and struck blindly at the panel of buttons on the lift wall. Somehow I managed to hit 'Open Door' and, after a second's hesitation, the doors moved apart again and I jumped out. That was when I heard footsteps on the nearby stairs. Someone was in a great hurry, half running, half jumping, and the clattering of their feet was getting rapidly louder.

By this time the lift was on the move again. The lights above it started blinking, and the footsteps were coming down faster than the lift was going up. Suddenly I decided to do what I was best at. I thrust open the entrance door and ran like a madman.

Even then, part of me was curious to know what the hell was going on: to stop under one of the lights and take a look at the piece of paper; to turn round and catch a glimpse of whoever was running after me – because, by now, I knew that's what they were doing. Behind me I'd heard the door open and feet pound on to the walkway. More than one pair by the sound of it. Fortunately, my feet kept thinking for me. On I ran, though I'd no idea where I was going. There seemed to be no way off that particular level.

Then suddenly I was at the top of some steps; and there was the lit-up church – which meant that a couple of flights down and just over to the left would be . . . yes, there it was: a large terrace and, behind it, the lights of the theatre foyer.

I was breathing heavily as I landed on the terrace, lost my balance for a moment and stumbled. Before I could straighten up I heard more footsteps, this time from the side and bearing down on me fast. At that point I was so confused I nearly turned round and ran straight back up the steps.

'Jefferies, what in God's name do you think you're playing at?'

Normally the dulcet tones of Mr Roberts getting annoyed don't appeal to me, but now I was so relieved to see him, they were music to my ears.

'Well?' he said, as I still hadn't answered his question.

'I got lost, sir,' I told him.

'Nothing like stating the obvious,' he said. 'Well, you score ten for honesty, nothing for imagination and bonus marks for sheer stupidity.'

'Yes, sir,' I agreed. 'Shall we go now?'

'What a good idea, Jefferies. I presume you'd like me to lead off.'

'Yes, sir. Thank you, sir.'

As we made our way through and out of the maze, I glanced round every now and then, but there was no sign of anyone following. No sound, either, except for Mr Roberts venting his annoyance: 'I waited ten minutes on the coach. Pure optimism, of course, but at the time it seemed preferable to carting the quarter of a mile back to the theatre. Honestly, if you didn't know the way back, why didn't you stick with one of the group?'

'They all left before me, sir.'

He lapsed into sullen silence for the rest of the walk. As we reached the coach the lads on the back seat saw us and started cheering. Old Roberts studiously avoided seeing the gestures a couple of them were making. 'Right, let's get you on board and be gone,' he said.

I took the applause and the jeering well enough. Even managed a little bow. Unfortunately, the only available seat was near the back, just in front of the lads, so the journey home was a bit of a trial. What annoyed me more than anything, though, was the fact that I couldn't take out the piece of paper while they were pestering me. In fact, it wasn't till I was home and getting ready for bed that I had a chance to look at it properly. It turned out to be a small piece of lined paper, with holes at the side, presumably out of something like a Filofax. And the only thing written on it was a series of numbers.

There were seven digits and, strange as it may seem, I didn't twig straight away what they meant. It was only as I was lying in bed that night that I realised it must be a London phone number. If you live outside London you get used to seeing the code in front, and whoever had written this had left the 01 off. The other thing that struck me then was that it ought to have been written in two blocks: three digits then four. This list of numbers was continuous, as if the writer had heard them spoken, rather than copying them from a directory.

Pure speculation, and probably idle speculation at that. But I spent a long time looking at that piece of paper before I turned the light off, till I not only knew the number by heart; I could picture every twist and flick of the pen, the tiny angled cross-bar on the seven. By the time I went to sleep I could have produced a perfect copy, even with my eyes closed.

The next day I found I couldn't concentrate too well on lessons. Old Roberts, predictably enough, had us discussing the previous night's performance. Did we feel the witches were presented as active forces of evil, rather than merely prophets of doom, etc. Normally I'd have joined in, and he must have realised my mind was elsewhere because he said, 'Feeling a little jaded today, Jefferies? Too much unaccustomed exercise last night, no doubt.' But he was so enthusiastic about his own ideas that he soon forgot me, and I was free to mull over my problem. Problems, rather. As I saw it, there were five.

One: why had I been given the piece of paper?

Two: what had happened to the man in the lift after I ran away?

Three: who had been running after me, and why?

Four: what was their connection with the man?

Five – and most important of all: what the hell was I supposed to do now?

As I couldn't answer any of the first four questions there seemed only one logical answer to the final one. But I didn't get round to making the call until late that evening. I had to wait till the rest of the family was safely occupied. It was just after nine forty.

As the ringing tone began my heart was beating at double speed. What exactly was I going to say, for heaven's sake? 'I'm phoning because a complete stranger gave me this number, and by the way can you tell me what's happened to him?' My nerve held out for ten rings, then I put the phone down. At least I'd tried. And perhaps my not getting through was an omen: 'Leave well alone; just screw up the piece of paper and throw it in the bin.'

But I didn't, and that night I hardly slept at all.

Next evening I tried again. This time it was earlier, and I was given no opportunity to change my mind. The phone at the other end was picked up almost immediately.

VOICE: Hello?
ME: Excuse me, but I think you might be able to help me. I was given your number by somebody.

101

VOICE:	(*Suspiciously*) This is an ex-directory number. Who gave it to you?
ME:	I don't know his name. I was hoping you could tell me because, well, the thing is, he seemed pretty ill when he gave it to me.
VOICE:	(*After a pause*) Ill?
ME:	Yes – at least he looked that way to me. I found him in a lift.
VOICE:	In the lift – yes, of course. Look, it's very thoughtful of you to phone like this. I should explain. It was my brother you met. He has a heart condition. Quite serious. In fact, he was very lucky the other night. We found him in time to get him to hospital. He's still there, otherwise I'm sure he'd want to thank you himself for phoning.
ME:	Oh – well, he's all right then?
VOICE:	Yes, yes. He'll need to rest, of course . . . I presume he gave you the number so you could call for help.
ME:	I'm afraid I didn't do too well then. I'm only two days late.
VOICE:	(*Laughing*) Not to worry. As it happened, things worked out fine.

As far as I was concerned, that should have been the end of the call, but he carried on talking to me for a while about nothing in particular, pointing out several times how grateful his brother would be. I was on my guard in case he said something like 'If you give me your number I'll get him to thank you personally.' But he didn't. Eventually, he stopped quite abruptly, said 'thank you' for the nth time, and put the phone down.

For the rest of the evening I paced round the house: the phone call had given me the creeps and I couldn't settle to anything. I suppose what I'd been told was just about plausible – if you discounted the running footsteps as coincidence – but one thing really bothered me. If, as he said, his brother had nearly died a couple of nights ago, the man I'd spoken to had no right to sound so calm about it. Relieved, yes; that I could have understood. But completely detached and emotionless? We could just as easily have been discussing the price of cheese, or how to polish a pair of shoes.

And how had I sounded to him? Hopefully, as if I believed him. That night I stayed up late, reading. When I finally put out the light it was two a.m. Even then, I slept badly.

All this was two nights ago, since when nothing has happened; not in the strict sense of the word. But I have two good reasons for worry. Firstly, I think I'm being watched.

Despite the insomnia, I've found I can get some sleep so long as I make myself physically exhausted. So, when the others are asleep, in the small hours of the morning, I very quietly leave the house and go for a long walk. And for two nights in a row there's been a car I've not seen before parked a little way down on the other side of the road. Someone's sitting in the driving seat and both times I've walked past he's been consulting a map or something. When I come back, about half an hour later, the car has gone.

Secondly, I discovered something in the paper

this morning – I've been keeping my eyes open for the past few days: a short article about some foreign journalist. Seems he's written various things his government doesn't like, they've put the screws on him and he's come to this country for some kind of safety. Now he's gone missing and nobody knows where. There's a rather blurred photograph too, not a particularly recent one either, but clear enough for me.

When I look back over what I've written in the last hour, what amazes me is how much you can write when it actually means something to you. As opposed to 'Macbeth: the Anatomy of Terror', which is what I should have been writing about.

Though, in a strange way, maybe I have."

It's that last remark which makes me question the whole thing. Provocative and tongue-in-cheek. Typical Jefferies. Give him any task and he'll find the most unusual way of doing it. Never orthodox. Never point A to point B like other people.

So what *has* he been writing about? The build-up of fear; the onset of paranoia, when everyone and everything is seen as threatening; the loss of reason and the torment of imagination. Well, they're all there in *Macbeth*, so maybe I should write: 'As a fictional foray into the realms of the disturbed mind, this is probably worthy of a place in the school magazine. As an examination of the text it is, as you well know, complete rubbish.' And having soothed his ego with the school magazine reference, I'd give him nought out of twenty.

So why don't I?

Partly because I'm in a unique position to verify the truth of much of his story. I was the one who went back to find him at the Barbican; he was certainly out of breath when I found him, and somewhat ill at ease; my remarks at the time are recorded more or less verbatim, as is my comment to him in the English lesson; on the two occasions I saw him subsequently he appeared tired and distant.

I realise, of course, that by embroidering a fictional tale with threads of fact, the whole thing is made to sound more believable – and he is a sophisticated enough boy to realise this also. The 'disappearing journalist' is also fact. I read it myself in the Sunday paper.

All this I can explain away, if with some difficulty. Two things remain.

Jefferies handed in his 'essay' yesterday, Monday. Today he was absent from my lesson and, as it transpired when I later checked the register, had been absent all day. More significant perhaps is the small piece of lined paper attached to his work. On it is written a sequence of numbers, in a hand that seems to me very different from Jefferies', judging by the figures used when dating his work, for example.

Therein, I suppose, lies the answer. If this is an elaborate hoax and Jefferies is having a bit of a laugh at my expense – at my gullibility – then the proof lies in the phone number.

I shall dial it and find out.

EENA, MEENA

Vivien Alcock

The platform was crowded. Edward was waiting for the train to Kentish Town, and not thinking of anything in particular. He did not notice the girl who was standing a little way back. She was waiting, too. She seemed nervous. Her eyes kept looking this way and that, as if she was afraid someone was watching her.

When he heard the train coming, Edward turned his head. Then it happened, so quickly – now he saw the train, now he didn't. Something blocked it out, something toppling forward with a shriek . . .

Edward grabbed the girl, or perhaps she grabbed him, he could never be certain afterwards. Oddly he felt no sense of danger. They hugged each other like lovers, while the train brushed past them and slowed to a stop. People getting out pushed them aside. People getting in stared at them, but only one woman said, 'What happened? Are you all right?' – and even she did not wait for an answer.

As the doors began to slide together, a thin, grinning boy shouted through the narrowing gap, 'It was all an ac— '

The door closed, shutting off the rest of what he was saying. Edward saw him making faces through the glass, now pulling up the corners of his wide mouth, now pushing them down. Then he and the train were gone, leaving Edward behind, still holding the girl. He could feel her trembling in his arms.

'What the hell did you think you were doing?' he demanded angrily, more shaken now than he had been when it was actually happening. 'If you want to kill yourself, you might at least do it in private. You nearly had us both over. I could be dead now!' His voice rose in indignation at the thought. Then he added gently, for she had raised her head and he saw that she was very pretty, 'I'm sorry. You'd better sit down.'

'Not here,' she said in a small voice, 'I want to get out of here. I need fresh air.'

'You need a drink,' he said, taking charge. 'Come on.'

She went with him meekly, up the escalator and into the windy street. Although it was not yet five o'clock, it was already getting dark. She clung to his arm as if for protection, and strands of her honey-gold hair blew across his face. He fancied other men looked at him enviously.

Poor kid, he thought, I wonder why she tried to kill herself? Pregnant, I bet, and afraid to tell her parents. Doesn't know what to do . . . Were there any girls left who didn't know what to do?

'How old are you?' he asked.

'Twenty-five,' she said.

Twenty-five! He'd thought her about sixteen. Immediately he felt young and gauche, and was afraid the publican would guess he was only seventeen, and refuse to serve him the brandy he'd planned to order for her. He was grateful when she said she'd prefer a coffee.

The pub was not yet crowded. They found a table in the corner and sat for a moment in silence. The girl wrapped her fingers round her cup as if trying to warm them. Edward was trying to think what to say. He was an only child, the son of elderly and conventional parents, and though he'd often longed for adventure, now it had come, he didn't know what to do with it. It was the girl who spoke first.

'I didn't jump,' she said, 'I was pushed.'

The platform had been crowded. 'It was all an accident.' Was that what the boy had been trying to tell him? Then she wasn't in trouble . . .

'I'm glad!' he blurted out, and blushed when she stared at him in astonishment. 'I mean, I'm glad you didn't try to kill yourself.'

'Someone,' she said, her voice high and clear, 'someone is trying to kill me.'

'*What*!'

Heads turned their way, and he added more quietly, 'It must've been an accident. People jostle— '

She treated this suggestion with scorn. 'Accident my eye,' she said. 'I tell you, I felt her hand on my back.'

'Her? You mean you know who it is?'

'Well, it's either her or him,' she said, with the air of someone trying to be fair. 'There isn't much choice. There're only two of them with a motive. I haven't got persecution mania, if that's what you're thinking.'

'No, of course not!'

'Besides, she's tried it before. This isn't the first time. Last week it was tennis-balls.'

'Tennis-balls?' Edward repeated, bewildered.

'Left them on the third stair from the top. One ball I might've accepted as an accident, but the stair was crowded with them. I could hear them bouncing all around me as I fell. There must've been a dozen, at least, but when I came round – I'd been knocked out – she said they could only find one. Where'd the others got to, that's what I'd like to know? And the bulb from the landing light—'

'Was that on the stair too?' Edward asked, confused.

She looked at him impatiently, as if wishing Fate had sent her an older and more intelligent rescuer.

'Someone had removed it so that the stairs would be dark and I wouldn't see the balls,' she explained. '*She* knew I was going to bed early. I had a cold. And so she rings the bell at eleven o'clock, pretending she's forgotten her key. Rings the bell knowing I'm alone in the house and it will bring me down. Then she sits on the steps and waits for Timothy to come home, pretending to be shut out.'

'How awful,' Edward said, but his voice sounded flat, inadequate for the occasion. His mind was full of bouncing tennis-balls and questions. If 'she', whoever she was, had waited on the front steps for Timothy, whoever he was, to return, when had she hidden the extra tennis-balls? He was afraid there might be a very simple answer to this question, so, not wanting to see the look of impatience on her face again, he did not

110

ask it. Instead he said, 'Why should she want to kill you?'

'It's a long story . . . ' She looked round and the people at the next table glanced quickly away, trying to pretend they'd not been listening, though their ears still quivered. 'Let's go,' she said, standing up.

Out in the street, she took Edward's arm again, and looked round nervously at the people passing, as if searching for someone she didn't want to see.

'I'm frightened,' she said. 'I keep thinking she may be waiting somewhere on the way home, that she'll try again.'

'I'll see you home,' Edward promised, and she smiled at him gratefully.

'Will you? I feel safe with you. Let's go by bus.'

They sat side by side in the back seat, their heads close together. He could smell the flowery scent on her hair and the faint peppermint of her breath. It seemed strange that so sweet a perfume should accompany the sour tale of greed and hate she told him.

Her name was Daphne Carter and she was an orphan. She and her two cousins, Timothy and Miranda, lived with their Uncle Robert, who was rich, childless – and dying. The three of them were his only heirs. If any one of them died before he did, their share would be equally divided between the survivors.

'So she knows she has to kill me before he dies. Otherwise it will be too late. She knows I'd never leave anything to her.'

'But if she has her own share, she wouldn't—' Edward began.

'You don't know her. She's greedy. She always was. She used to hide our chocolates when we were little and eat them in her bed at night. Besides, she hates me. She's afraid Timothy is sweet on me and she's jealous.'

'Why don't you go to the police?' Edward asked.

'How can I? I've no evidence. It's just my word against hers. Besides, I don't want them coming round asking questions. It would kill Uncle Robert. The doctors said anything, any excitement or commotion . . . It's his heart, you see. The doctors say he can't last . . . ' Her voice shook and she turned her head away quickly.

He put his arm around her and held her close, and tried desperately to think of some way of helping her. The bus moved slowly through the rush-hour traffic, stopping and starting, and he wished the journey would never end. She was safe at the moment in his arms. Her head rested against his shoulder as she told him softly of the other attempts on her life: the heavy bronze jar falling from the chest on the landing, showering her with water and leaves, crashing on to the tiles by her feet, then the unseen hands in the swimming pool, pulling her down by the ankles . . .

'Couldn't you see who it was?' he asked.

'I'm short-sighted,' she confessed. 'I was choking and my eyes were full of water.'

'You mustn't go back! Not while she's there. Come home with me,' he said impulsively, and had a quick vision of his parents' astonished faces, seeing him bring a young woman out of the night. He seemed to hear her story through their ears and was dismayed to find how incredible it sounded. He

112

was relieved when she shook her head and said she didn't want to leave her uncle.

'They let him come home from the hospital yesterday,' she told Edward. 'He said he wanted to die in his own bed. There's a nurse with him. Miranda won't try anything while she's there. I'll be safe at home now.'

They got off the bus and walked hand in hand through the darkening streets until they came to a tall Victorian house on the corner of Well Walk. She stopped and looked up at the lighted window on the first floor.

'Uncle Robert's awake,' she said. 'I must go in.'

'Shall I come with you?'

She hesitated, then said, 'No. I want to sit with him and he's not allowed other visitors. Only the family.'

'Daphne, don't go!' he cried, feeling a sudden panic. 'I don't want you to go. Supposing I never see you again? Let me come in with you. I won't disturb your uncle. I'll just lie outside your door all night like a guard dog.'

'What would the night nurse think? No. I'll bolt my door and be safe enough . . . ' She hesitated, and added slowly, 'You could do something for me, though.'

'Anything,' he said.

'It sounds silly, but – could you write down what happened on the platform, and the other things I've told you? Then I can tell her it's on record and she won't dare try again.'

He promised, and she kissed him lightly on the mouth. 'Thank you.'

113

'Oh,' he said, not wanting to let go of her hands, 'I'm frightened for you.'

But she pulled away and ran up the steps to the front door.

'When can I come again?' he called. 'Tomorrow? Early? Can I come to breakfast?'

'All right,' she said, laughing, and let herself into the house. Edward stood for a long time, staring at the house where she lived, unable to tear himself away. He saw a shadow against the curtains of the window on the first floor, and thought they parted a little, as if someone was looking out. He waved, but couldn't see if anyone waved back.

He waited and after a short time, heard the front door open. He moved forward eagerly, and then stopped. It was a different girl who came running down the stairs. She had short dark hair cut in a fringe, and in spite of the cold wind, was wearing only a green sweatshirt, jeans and grubby white trainers. She glanced at him curiously but would have walked by if he hadn't said quickly, 'Excuse me . . . '

'Yes?'

'Are you Miranda?' he asked, suddenly doubtful, for she looked so young, hardly more than a child.

'Yes. Why? I don't know you, do I?'

'My name's Edward Blake. I'm a friend of your cousin's.'

'You're in luck, then,' she said, 'she's in. Came back a few minutes ago.' She jerked her thumb at the house. 'Try the bell.'

'It's you I want to talk to,' he said.

'Me?'

'I want to talk to you about Daphne. About what

happened this afternoon. She told me everything, and we made a record of it and posted it to my home,' he added untruthfully.

She scratched her head, and shivered. 'What are you on about? I'm not with you. Is this going to take long, only it's cold out here. Let's go back into the house. Or there're cafés in Heath Street, if you don't want Daphne to know about whatever it is.'

He went with her. In the café she asked for hot chocolate and a currant bun. 'I'm always hungry,' she said.

A greedy girl, Daphne had called her, but she wasn't fat. With a chocolate moustache and a cheek bulging with bun, she looked more than ever like a child.

'How old are you?' he asked, as he had asked her cousin.

'Mind your own business,' she told him. 'What's all this about Daphne and a record? I didn't borrow it, if that's what she thinks.'

'Not that sort of record. A written one. I put down everything she told me, and everything I knew myself. I was there, you see, when you tried to kill her. I was the one who saved her.'

'*What!*'

'I suppose you couldn't very well wait to see what happened. Did you think you'd got away with it? You must've had a shock when she came back.'

She stared at him. A crumb had stuck to the corner of her mouth and she licked it away. She looked puzzled, but ready to laugh if it turned out to be some sort of joke.

'It was rather a blow,' she said cheerfully. 'I thought

I'd done her in proper and she pops up again, large as life. Not a spot of blood on her . . . How did I do it, by the way?'

'You can't laugh this off,' he said, but his voice lacked conviction. 'It's not your first attempt, is it? There were the tennis-balls . . . '

It was no good. He couldn't believe it of her. She was the sort of girl he felt at home with. An ordinary girl. She could've gone to his school, or been the younger sister of one of his friends. A girl who would hit a tennis-ball into the net and laugh, not arrange a murderous booby trap on a dark stair.

'Tennis-balls?' she repeated, staring at him. 'Are you talking about the time she fell downstairs? She blamed me. Said I must've left a tennis-ball on the stairs. We did find one behind the umbrella stand in the hall, but it wasn't mine. It was an old one, absolutely filthy!'

'You said "we". Who else was there?'

'Tim. My brother. Why do you look like that? You can't seriously think we tried to kill her with a tennis-ball? I believe you do? I really believe you do! It's too Agatha Christie for words.'

'There was also the bronze urn,' he said angrily.

She rocked back in her seat and laughed, like a happy child. People looked at her and smiled in sympathy. Even Edward felt his lips twitch.

But it wasn't a joke, he remembered. He had been there on the platform. He had seen her try to push her cousin under the train . . .

No! Of course he hadn't! What did I see exactly? he wondered, I must try and remember. I was standing

116

there, a safe distance from the edge, as I always do. Heard the train coming. Turned my head and saw Daphne falling forward . . . Falling? Her hands had clutched him but not pulled him off balance. He hadn't even rocked on his feet. He felt no sense of danger. Could she have faked it? Lunged forward like a fencer, put on an act . . .

'It was all an act.' Was that what the boy had been trying to tell him? Making faces through the glass like the masks of comedy and tragedy at a theatre?

'I don't know,' he said aloud. 'I don't know what to believe.'

'Poor Edward,' Miranda said. 'Has Daphne been playing her tricks on you? You mustn't mind. She's an awful liar. You can't believe a word she says.'

'But why? Why pick on me?' Edward saw his own reflection in the mirror behind her. Was this the face a beautiful stranger would want to see at breakfast? He sighed. It was already beginning to seem like a dream; beauty falling out of the night into his arms, the sweet scent of honey-gold hair, the soft, peppermint kiss on his lips, the strange tale.

'I suppose you haven't really got a rich uncle, dying in his own bed.'

'Yes, we have,' she said, her face suddenly becoming dutifully grave, like a good child at a funeral. 'And I don't think you ought to joke about him. Poor Uncle Robert. I must be going.'

'And is he rich?' Edward asked, frowning. 'Has he left his money to be divided between the three of you?'

'I suppose Daphne told you. She would. Money's her god. She's always been greedy.'

'That's what she said about you.'

'Me?' She saw him looking at her empty plate and flushed. 'I'm still growing. I have to eat a lot. I'm not as old as she is. I'll pay, if that's what's worrying you.'

'No, I'll pay,' he said firmly.

They left the café together and walked in silence through the narrow side streets till they reached the tall Victorian house on the corner of Well Walk. They both looked up at the window on the first floor. The curtains had been drawn back and there was no light showing.

'His eyes get tired reading,' Miranda said. 'He says he likes to lie and watch the stars, but I expect he's fallen asleep.'

'Couldn't the nurse read to him?'

'She may have popped out for something when Daphne came in. Or she may be down in the kitchen. I dunno.'

Edward felt a growing sense of uneasiness. It was a big house, on three floors, a house to get lost in.

'Don't go in,' he said. 'I've got a feeling . . . oh, that something's going to happen. Can't you stay with a friend tonight?'

'You're crazy.'

'I think Daphne must hate you. She told me you were trying to kill her for her share of your uncle's money. I'm not joking. It's true. She asked me to write it down so that it could be used in evidence.'

'Mad or drunk,' she said, walking backwards up

118

the steps to the front door. 'Why don't you go home and put your head in a bucket of cold water?'

'Have you made your will?' he asked, but she only laughed, and let herself into the house, shutting the door behind her.

A light showed through the fanlight, but otherwise the house was in darkness. He peered through the letter-box but saw only an empty hall. Miranda had vanished. Probably the main rooms were at the back but there was no way through to the garden. He thought of the old man dying on the first floor, the young girl laughing about the tennis-balls and the beautiful stranger catching him in a web of honey-gold hair. Why had she chosen him for her schemes? Because of his gullible face?

A horrible picture was forming in his mind, like a picture in a dark mirror. It was not Daphne who was to be murdered by Miranda, but the reverse. Miranda, whose next-of-kin was her brother not her cousin, must not be allowed to inherit her share of her uncle's money. Somehow she was to be murdered in a way that would make it look as if Daphne herself was the intended victim.

How could that be done? 'Why don't you borrow my coat, Miranda? It's a cold night. And now my headscarf . . . That's right. Why don't you walk in the dark street, Miranda, looking like me? So that the police will think your stupid brother killed the wrong girl, and I will get the lot.'

Was that her plan?

And I, poor fool, Edward thought bitterly, my part was to be the star witness: 'Yes, I was there when they tried to push Daphne under the train. I

119

saw it all. I was the one who saved her. Yes, I have it all written down, look— '

He rang the bell furiously, and when no one answered, hammered at the door.

'Miranda! Let me in! Let me in! It's you who's going to be murdered! Miranda!'

A chink of light appeared between the curtains of the window on his left. He saw a pale hand, a shadowed face, a strand of bright hair.

'Daphne? Is that you?' he shouted, his voice echoing wildly in the narrow street. 'Don't touch her! It's too late. I know you mean to kill her. Do you hear? I know everything, and I'll tell!'

The chink of light disappeared. Above him, he heard a window open and he looked up. A shadowy figure with white hair and striped pyjamas stared down at him. An old man's voice demanded angrily, 'What the devil do you think you're— '

The voice broke off abruptly. The old man grunted and clutched at his chest. He stood for a moment, gasping and swaying, then he slowly crumpled, like a piece of paper being crushed by an invisible hand. In the ghastly silence that followed, Edward saw the light go on in the room. A woman in a nurse's uniform hurried towards the window.

Terrified, he turned and ran like a criminal down the dark street.

The old man's death was reported in *The Times*:

CARTER. On October 16th, peacefully at his home, Robert William Carter. Beloved uncle of Daphne, Timothy and Miranda . . . No flowers by request.

I have killed an old man, Edward thought, I have saved an innocent girl and let a murderous one go free. But will I ever know, for certain, which girl was which?

THE STEEL FINGER
John Gordon

No one has ever called me a thief, said the man on the train. No one ever will. The word does not fit me, and what I am telling you now is for your ears only and then it will drift away on the air and be lost for ever. I know I can trust you, for you are hardly different from me, and you know better than to brand a person without proof. And there is no evidence. None.

The train throbbed and hummed its way through the night, rattled occasionally, then lowered its head to the rails and gathered speed again, heading north, putting London behind it. The compartment was almost empty and the man who was speaking had put his briefcase on the seat beside him, unbuttoned his overcoat, and sat with his hands loosely clasped on the table between us.

He was young, but I was much younger and I was in his debt for saving me from an embarrassing situation. Only an hour ago he had appeared at my shoulder in the buffet at Liverpool Street Station at the very moment when the barman, sure I was under age, was about to turn me away. But then this stranger was suddenly addressing me as an old friend, paying for my drink and leading me away. Of course, I was then in worse trouble as I was only seventeen, alone in the big city, and had now been picked up by a stranger – a man. But he had seen what was in my mind and had said, 'You were about to be caught, and all I did was rescue you. So it's one lager and farewell. No strings.'

I had believed him and we began to talk. Perhaps that was what he wanted, to talk, but I have never understood why he chose to tell me so much. He was too calm and too much in control of himself to need to make a confession, especially to someone of my age, and he did not appear to be the type of man who had to increase his self-esteem by boasting.

He wore a light grey suit, a white shirt, a neat tie. He was tall, fair, and I am sure he was quite good-looking although I cannot, for the life of me, now recall his face. He was so anonymous he must have had a genius for camouflage. Perhaps that evening, as one law-breaker to another, he was challenging me to remember him.

The first time I took anything that did not belong to me, he said, I found it incredibly easy.

I was fifteen and I was buying a key-ring from the shop at the petrol station just along the road from my school. You know what those places are like. Everyone used to pile in at lunchtimes for crisps and stuff, and it was always crowded with motorists and kids. The girl behind the counter was kept pretty busy, so I had to queue with the key-ring and the money in my hand and it was going to take ages. Suddenly my patience ran out. I turned away and went back to the shelf to put the key-ring back – but I didn't do it. I walked out with it in my pocket. I didn't even think; I just did it – rather like that incident in the bar just now.

Of course I wasn't the only one. Every day you used to see people come swarming out of that place grinning at what they'd got stuffed up their sleeves. And boasting about it.

'What have you got, John?' they asked me.

'Nothing,' I said. 'I don't believe in it – taking things that aren't yours.'

'You must be mad.'

'I can't help that,' I said. 'That's the way I am.'

He continued to speak as the train rocked on through the night, and as he got deeper into his story he seemed to become younger, as though every word was taking him back to the time when it all happened. He was fifteen again and had just stepped out of the shop with the key-ring in his pocket.

We were walking between the petrol pumps, several of us, with Gary, my best friend, and there was this girl, Dawn something. I only sort of knew her at that time. She had a lot of hair, curling around everywhere, down to her shoulders, and you could hardly see her face, but what you could see wasn't bad. If she had pushed her hair back, I thought, she might have been kind of startling, but at that moment it was just her mouth I noticed. Her lips were a little round ring as if she was whistling – but that wasn't what she was doing. She was sucking in her breath because something had surprised her. I caught her just at that very moment. Her eyes couldn't avoid mine, and then I knew. We both knew. She had seen what I'd done in the shop, and she'd heard me deny it. That's what had surprised her.

I kept my eyes on her, and I spoke very clearly. 'I think,' I said, 'that it's absolutely stupid to nick things.' She began to blush, but I wouldn't let her look away. 'It pays to be honest,' I said. 'Absolutely honest.'

Her blush did not last long. Now she was pale. 'I didn't take anything either,' she said very quietly, as if she was out of breath, and I knew she was telling me she was not going to give me away, so I let her lower her eyes and hide in her hair.

'I got a new name for you,' Gary said to me. 'Honest John, who never nicks nothing.'

I smiled a bit, as though I wasn't as pure as all that, and I let him burble on because I was thinking. Partly about that girl. She wore black tights and a shortie skirt as if she was a real goer, but there was something about the way she walked with her knees close together, awkward as a little kid, that was a dead giveaway. She was only playing at it. So I wasn't bothered about her, except that she'd seen me.

That was a problem. Until that moment, I had been walking between the petrol pumps and feeling pretty clever. I had my key-ring and I still had my money; I'd done it without a thought in my head and I'd got away with it. I felt so good it was just as though a door had opened and I'd been pushed through into the sunlight. I hadn't only seen how easy it was, I'd also seen how I could do it again and again and get

126

better at it. I knew I had the talent for it, and I was full of power and joy and everything else – except that someone had seen me. I couldn't get that off my mind, but I kept on talking.

'You know what's going to happen,' I said. 'They're going to spoil it.'

'Spoil what?' said Gary. 'Who?'

'All the thickies,' I said. 'Showing off about what they've nicked. They're going to have to stop or get caught.'

'So what? I thought you were against thieving, Honest John.'

'I am. It's immoral.' There were just the three of us now. The girl had tagged along, keeping quiet just like a kid who has been told off but wants to get back in your good books. I looked directly at her. 'And nicking doesn't work,' I said. 'Does it?'

She knew it was a challenge. 'I don't know,' she said very quietly.

I slowed down until she was almost, but not quite, level with me, and I spoke so softly that only she could hear. 'That's okay, Dawn,' I said. 'Don't worry about it.'

She was so surprised to hear me say her name that her head jerked up and she smiled straight at me, but then she went red and hid in her hair again. I knew then, in that moment, that she would never ever tell anyone what she knew. She was mine, I felt great.

When we got into school we were separated in the crush of bodies flying off everywhere. I didn't even notice her go, but Gary said, 'She's still looking at you, John. I think she fancies you.'

I just shrugged.

127

'Don't blame you,' he said. 'She's not much.'

I could have hit him, because it wasn't up to him to say what I felt about anybody, but I just kept walking. I had a lot to think about.

A kind of miracle had happened, and I had to sort out what it meant. When I put that key-ring into my pocket there'd been a flash inside my head because it was so easy, and in that split second I could also see ahead. I saw I could always take what I wanted, because things were spread about everywhere, in shops and desks and store cupboards, lying about like grass in a field. It was just as natural for me to take what I wanted as it was for an animal to eat the grass.

'I'm a sheep,' I said suddenly, just to keep Gary quiet about the girl. 'I go where I like and I eat what I like and nobody can tell I've been there.'

He didn't understand me, of course, but he bleated like a sheep, doing his best to be funny.

'And I don't bleat,' I said. 'I don't make a sound. I'm a silent sheep.' That was one of the things I'd seen more clearly than anything – you never bragged in my trade; my new trade – and I turned my back on Gary so he wouldn't ask me any more questions.

'Have it your own way,' he said, but he still followed me.

There was one chink in my armour, of course, and she was waiting for me at the end of the day in the corridor. It was winter and already getting dark. She was in a bit of a shadow but I could see her quite easily so it was stupid the way she behaved. She waited till Gary and me had got past her and then she lunged forward, stuck out her arm and said,

'A girl wants me to give you this.' I took something from her hand and then, as if it was the greatest secret ever, she'd spun around and run away.

'What've you got there?' said Gary.

It was a note, but it had been folded over so many times it was a little square wad of paper. Even when I opened it out it was very tiny, and so was the writing, so I had to step under one of the lights to read it. It was a very short note. What it said was: 'I'll never tell anybody. Never. Never.' It wasn't signed, not even an initial.

Gary wanted to see it, but I wouldn't let him. 'It's not from her,' I said. 'It's from someone else.'

'I can't understand it,' he said. 'Who'd look at you?'

'Wrong again,' I told him. 'The point is: would I look at her?' I glanced down at the note. It had nobody's name on it, but there was a cross for a kiss – except that it had been almost rubbed away as if she had been far too frightened to let me know how she felt but hadn't been able to prevent herself leaving just a shadow of it. That was why she'd run away so fast.

'What're you smiling at?' said Gary, but he knew I wasn't going to tell him.

If he'd kept his eyes open he'd have guessed what it was all about, because she followed us when we got outside. She lagged behind so she could always pretend she was going somewhere else, but I saw her. It was very childish. I only glanced back when we crossed a road but she was always there, so when Gary went his own way home, I slowed up until she came level.

'Thanks for your note,' I said.

129

'That's all right.' I could hardly hear her, and it was so dark I couldn't see her face. I held out my hand. 'Here,' I said. 'I've got something for you.'

Her fingers were cold and trembling so much I had to make sure she didn't drop the key-ring I gave her. Then she tried to hand it back. 'No,' she said. 'I don't want it.'

'Is that because I didn't pay for it?'

'I didn't mean that.' She was so startled that her head came up and I saw her face. Girls sometimes put you off because they know too much, but she wasn't like that. She was like a kid who'd been hurt. 'Honest!' she said. 'I didn't mean it like that, John.'

Any second she'd be crying, so I said, 'I got it for you, anyway.' We both knew it was a lie, but that made it better somehow. 'I took a risk for it,' I said.

'I know.' A streetlight caught her eyes and made them sparkle. She was wild with a sort of excitement I couldn't understand. 'I'll keep it for ever,' she said, and she clasped her hands under her chin as though she was holding it to her heart. Crazy, but I knew what I had to do. There was no one near enough to see, so I kissed her.

'Oh!' she said. Her cheeks were smooth and cold. 'Oh, John!' she said, but even her lips were cold and I didn't want to kiss her again, so I told her that people were watching.

I took her home. She lived in a grotty little street, and I knew she wanted me to kiss her again when we got there, but I made as if I was too nervous, and that was something she understood very well so she went skittering into the passageway alongside her house just as if Christmas had come early.

I discovered that I was smiling, but I wasn't too happy. I didn't like the risks I'd taken, not even for Dawn Dewhurst.

After that day I paid for everything I got at the garage shop. Anyway there wasn't much choice because it was just as I said – the thickies spoiled it. A notice went up on the door and only two school kids were allowed in at a time, so nicking stopped being a popular sport and was left to the specialists. That did not include me – I wasn't going to be known as one of *them*. They wanted people to admire them for their nerve, so they had to let everybody know who they were, which wasn't my style. But I was really glad to know who they were – so I could steer clear. What I needed was technique. Technique.

He patted the table, emphasising the word. The train gave a lurch, but he didn't notice it.

Technique came very slowly because I was in no hurry. Patience is something I have plenty of, so I kept my eyes open and waited. It wasn't very long before I thought I recognised every store detective in the city, even when they moved from shop to shop. Not that this did me much good because there's always the chance of a new one coming in, so I became more and more cautious. And then there were the hidden TV cameras: I didn't like the thought of them at all, even though I was pretty sure I'd spotted most of them. It all began to seem so difficult that I was tempted to do what had worked so well in the first

131

place – grab and get out. But what if I was stopped outside the shop with something with its price tag still on, no receipt, and a glaring gap on the shelf near where I'd been standing?

It was beginning to seem hopeless when, one day, in the basement of the biggest store in the city, I saw something that opened the door for me. Once again it happened in a flash, but this time I'd been working steadily towards it so when I saw a man in overalls flattening cardboard boxes and tying them in bundles I was ready for it. It was the way he cut the string. When I saw that, I knew he was showing me how I could take something from a shop, walk out with it quite safely, and without leaving an empty space on the shelf. Safe. Very safe.

It was the speed he was tying up the bundles that gave me the clue. He was using a large ball of thick string and, each time he finished tying a bundle, the string seemed to cut itself without him doing anything at all. I watched, but all I could see at first was that he seemed to brush the string with his knuckles and it obligingly cut itself and allowed him to toss the bundle aside. Then, quite suddenly, I saw how he did it. His knuckles were not bare. He had a ring on one finger, but it wasn't for decoration. It had a tiny hooked blade attached to it and all he had to do was to slash at the string, a bit like a fighting cock, I suppose, and the little spur bit it through.

That was all, but it was enough. I didn't see how I could get one of those rings, and anyway it would not have been precisely what I needed. It just gave me the idea. I made myself a steel finger.

In the art room at school we used those thin knives

that have snap-off blades, so it was easy to get a piece of one. They are sharp, so I had to be careful, but I found that I could tape a piece of blade along the back of my finger so that it lay snug and tight and gave me a fingernail like a razor. I practised a lot in my bedroom and found that the blade had to be taped uncomfortably tight before it was useful, but it did what I wanted and I was ready.

One day I gave Gary the slip after school and got to the city centre on my own. The Christmas lights hung over the streets and everywhere was crowded, which suited me well but I was still cautious. And I was so honest it shone. I carried nothing to hide things in, my windcheater was zipped up, and the hand that wore a fingerstall was held high against my chest because it was obviously painful.

I chose the store with the best stationery department. There was a big display of pens and I stood there for a while, looking at the racks on the wall. I'd made up my mind what I was going to have before I touched anything, and when I moved I was as near certain as I could be that no camera eye was on me and that nobody was watching – not that it would matter too much even if they were. I reached out to the pen I wanted. It was on one of those display cards with a plastic front, sealed tight. It hung on a rod with others behind it, and when I reached for it I grasped two, one behind the other, and then lifted my injured hand as though to help unhook it.

I pressed the tip of my wounded finger into the backing card of the second pen and felt the blade pierce the stitching of the fingerstall, as I knew it would. Then I pressed harder until the tip of my steel finger cut through the card and I ran it all the way down, keeping up the pressure. When the slit was long enough I pushed my thumb through and prised the pen into my palm. The plastic facing crackled, but I did not look round to see if anyone had heard. Instead, I breathed a sigh and dropped my hands as though I had decided that this pen was not for me.

As my hands went down, the pen in my palm slipped easily into the pocket of my jeans and I lifted my injured hand, palm outwards, wincing very slightly as I did so. Nothing was missing from the display, the top pen was still visible, and I stooped towards the cheap pens near the floor and chose one, holding it in the open as I went to the counter to pay for it.

I didn't see her until I turned around. She gave a little start and her mouth opened as if she was surprised to see me, but she blushed at the same time, smiled and turned jerkily away and joined the queue at the till. I didn't believe in her surprise. She had been following me again.

There was anger in me, quite a lot, but I didn't let it show. I wanted to walk out, get away from there, leave her behind, but that would have been a bad move. I had to know how much she knew, so I stood alongside her as she fumbled with the Christmas cards and little notebooks she was buying. At least it gave me the chance to look around. Nobody was paying us the least attention.

'Your poor finger,' she said. 'What have you done?'

Her voice was so soft I had to lean forward so that my face touched her hair and she almost drew away, but not quite. She was being daring.

'I caught my knuckles in a door,' I said. 'It's not broken. This comes off soon.' I held my hand in front of her, and in that instant we both saw that something had gone wrong. I had forgotten to adjust the fingerstall, and a centimetre of steel glinted at the end of my finger.

She moved much faster than was necessary. All I had to do was turn my hand over and the blade was out of sight, but she snatched at it and covered it with her own clenched fist.

I heard her draw in her breath sharply as she grasped the blade, but her hand over mine did not even tremble. She clutched my finger and held on, even when the till was in front of us and she had to put her cards on to the counter. Now she needed her purse and she would have to release my finger. I knew it wasn't sweat I felt in her palm. She was bleeding.

I can act quite well in a crisis. I used her blood as a disguise. 'My knuckle!' I said, and winced. 'Look what's happened.' I freed my hand from hers and held it up. The fingerstall was bloody and I nursed my hand while the girl at the till sucked in her breath and gave me all her sympathy while Dawn, clutching at a handkerchief, paid quickly, and we walked out together.

The cut in her palm was deep. 'You needn't have done that,' I said.

She was so pale I thought she might faint, so I let her cling to my arm as we walked slowly under the Christmas lights, and after a while I asked her if she was feeling better.

'Yes, thank you,' she said, just as if she was a little kid thanking me for a chocolate. But then

135

she was alarmed again, and she cried out, 'I thought somebody was going to see!'

'Nobody did,' I said. 'Nobody but you.'

'Thank goodness!'

'It's all right,' I told her. 'Nothing's going to happen. I'm in the clear. Nobody saw what I did except you.'

'But I didn't see anything except the knife, John.' She was shaking her head. 'I don't know what you did with it.'

She was not lying. She never would lie. 'Promise you'll say nothing,' I said, 'and I'll tell you.'

'I promise.'

'It was an experiment. I just wanted to see if I could do it.' I told her what I'd done. I showed her the pen. 'You can have it,' I said. I didn't have any immediate use for it.

'No.' She put it back in my pocket. 'It's yours.'

'Not mine.' I looked directly into her face, and took a chance. 'It belongs to the shop,' I said.

'No.' Her hair moved on her shoulder as she shook her head. 'You took all the risk. It's yours.'

I stopped and held her cut hand in mine. A few minutes ago she would have been unable to keep her eyes steady as I looked at her, but now she gazed back at me, fiercely, defying me to back down and pretend I had not stolen the pen.

'It's yours!' She thrust her face close to mine. It was bright under the lights, people were jostling around us, but she defied them, too. 'You took it because you wanted it!'

Now she was trembling. Her eyes were a very pale blue, and they were wide and they shone so brightly

136

it was me who had to draw back. She would shout it out in a moment, and people would notice.

I kept my voice down. 'Yes,' I said, and began to walk, drawing her with me. 'That's what I do. I take what I want. Nobody is going to tell me what to do.'

I wanted her to be rational, but she had too much passion for that. 'John doesn't care!' she cried. 'John does what he likes! He's free!'

Heads turned our way. I tried to calm her by walking more quickly and agreeing with her. 'You're right,' I said. 'Being free is all that matters. I don't care about anything or anybody,' and then I paused, and said, 'Except . . . '

I wanted her to understand what I meant without having to say it. Any other girl I'd ever met would have known what I meant, but she couldn't see I was paying her a compliment. Oh no – she was simply too modest to understand.

'Except what?' she said.

I closed my eyes and laughed. 'You,' I said. 'I was talking about you. Dawn is the only one I care about.'

And then she surprised me again. Tears spilled from her eyes, and she turned and ran away from me.

In the train he drummed his fingers on the table, deep in thought, before he went on. I thought he was going to tell me more about the girl, but I was wrong.

Pens and key-rings were never going to be enough, and most other things were too bulky for my methods. But there is one small article that has value in itself

137

– and I'm not talking about gold or diamond rings. They can be traced. But *money* is anonymous. Money is the stuff that matters. Jewels have to be turned into money before they're of any use to you, and that means bringing in someone else. Do that, and, sooner or later, you're finished. It's got to be money.

So I told no one, not even Dawn – especially not Dawn. In fact we were never even seen together, I made sure of that. We met, of course, but always somewhere out of the way. The fact that we had secret meeting places appealed to her, and one of them was in the Cathedral Close.

I was heading there one dark Saturday afternoon very close to Christmas and taking in some of the city streets on the way when I stopped outside a second-hand bookshop – for no reason; I didn't even want a book, and I knew the only ones worth having were kept behind glass anyway. It was in Willow Hill, a part of the city where tourists go because it's old and picturesque and hidden away, and Miller's bookshop is just the sort of place you'd expect to find down there.

Inside, there were stacks of books everywhere, piled high on an old counter down the middle, heaped up around Mr Miller's desk, even on the floor, so it was like picking your way through a maze. I think what made me step inside was that there was nobody at the desk by the window and I could see that the cash drawer of the old wooden till was not properly closed. Of course I walked straight by it because there were several people browsing along the shelves, and I became one of them. I just buried myself in a book and kept my eyes open.

Then a door hidden away somewhere at the back of the shop opened and closed suddenly and Mr Miller came around a corner. He was talking to a woman who was obviously his wife, and it was she who went to the desk while he buttoned up his overcoat and went out, promising to be back in an hour.

There was no point in me being there any longer and I was about to browse my way towards the front when a chink of light in a dark corner at the back made me pause. The door they had just come through was not properly closed and a light was still on in the room beyond.

The shop was L-shaped, and the door was around the corner, out of sight of the desk. It was a bad arrangement – for them, but not for me. The shop had almost emptied, and I was alone at the back. I edged closer to the door and pushed it gently until it swung further open. I was looking into an office, but a very small one, no bigger than a cubby-hole and more untidy than the shop itself. There was a desk with a kettle on it, heaps of bills, notes pinned to shelves that were already overflowing with papers and books, a woman's coat on a hanger, an umbrella and a grey filing cabinet. I took it all in, but it was the cabinet that interested me. Mrs Miller's handbag lay on top of it.

I heard her talking to a man, and I calculated that he and I were the only two customers left in the shop. Three steps took me to the handbag, five seconds was all it took me to open it and lift out the purse. Three seconds more and the bag was back on the cabinet, and I had gone out and quietly pulled the door so that it was almost, but not quite, closed. All this time I had been listening and had heard the rustle of paper as Mrs Miller put the customer's book in a bag. Then I heard her counting his change and I was ready when she shut the drawer of the till. At exactly that moment I eased the door its last fraction of an inch, and the click of the latch was lost in the rattle of the till.

I went back along the shelves, looking at a book or two in full view of the desk, although luckily she was busy and hardly glanced my way, and then I wandered out but lingered to look in the window, utterly innocent.

I waited until I was around the corner before I opened the purse. There was twenty-five pounds in notes, but that was not important. Nor were the credit cards – I would never use them anyway – nor was the dentist's appointment, but the library tickets were different. They were what I needed because, mixed up with some loose change, there was a key, and only the library tickets told me what door it would open. The tickets had Mrs Miller's address.

Dawn was waiting for me in one of the little alleyways that led off the Close. It was already getting dark and I had to hold the key up to her face before she could see what it was.

'Give me your hand,' I said.

She did so, and I put the key in her bandaged palm and pressed her fingers over it. 'Now turn around,' I ordered. When she was facing me again, I put my arms around her. 'You've turned the key,' I said, 'so now we're locked together.'

It was exactly the right sort of thing to say to her, I

knew that, and when we kissed it was fierce. Nobody
was there to see us, and she put her head on my chest
so that we couldn't look at each other and she began
to whisper how much she loved me. She had never
dared say so much, and she was trembling.

'You and me,' I said into her hair. 'And nobody
knows.'

'Nobody!' She was fierce again. 'Because we're
not the same as anybody who ever lived!'

That was the moment to tell her. 'We're different,'
I said. 'The key proves it.'

'Key?' She had forgotten it already.

'It's our key,' I said, 'because I took a risk for
it.' I told her what had happened, detail by detail,
and she held herself stiffly, listening. I finished, but
she remained silent, so I said, 'I took it because of
you.'

Suddenly she tilted her head and looked me straight
in the face. 'Because of me?'

'You said we were free – not like other people,
not like shopkeepers.' Her eyes were searching my
face as I spoke. 'And I wanted the danger,' I said.
'For you.'

Then she was on fire again, defying everything
and everybody, but I pretended not to be aware of
it. 'Now I'm going to prove it to you,' I said, and
I took the key from her and held it before her eyes.
'I'm going to use it while you keep watch.'

I began to walk away, but she snatched at my
arm and spun me round. 'No!' she cried. 'Let me
do it!'

'I can't.'

'Yes! You took the key – I will use it!' There was

141

so much passion in her that she was clawing at my arm, pleading with me to release the key. Her hair was like a wild woman's and her eyes implored me to agree with her or the world would end. 'Please!' she begged. 'I have to do it. It's necessary!'

So I put the key in her hand.

The house was not far away, and we went there separately. It was in one of those quiet roads you don't expect to find in the centre of a city. There were long front gardens that didn't have cars parked in them, so you knew there were garages at the back, and you could tell from the pictures and lampshades you could see from the road that nothing was cheap.

I was ahead of her and walked past the Millers' house. It was so dark now that the streetlights had come on, but there were no lights within the house. It was empty.

The lamps in the street were old-fashioned, quite a distance apart and not bright, so I had to walk until I was almost beneath one before I could make the signal. All I had to do was to take my hands from the pockets of my windcheater and clasp them behind my back. I did so, but I did not look back until I was in shadow again.

I saw her go through the gate. I winced as it shut behind her with a clatter, but she didn't even bother to turn her head. She walked swiftly up the path to the front door as if she owned the place, and I moved on.

I had to keep watch, but I could not simply stand there while somebody, somewhere, observed me from behind a curtain, so I walked on as far as I could, and I timed her by imagining what she was doing. In my mind I saw her ring the doorbell, listen for footsteps inside the house and then, if nothing stirred, put the key in the lock and enter.

I reached the end of the road. Now she would be swiftly searching the ground floor for a bureau, pull open its drawers and feel inside.

I crossed the road. She must be upstairs by now. I'd told her where to look. The chest of drawers in the first bedroom. The top of the wardrobe.

I walked slowly, just fast enough not to be suspicious. There were a few parked cars, sometimes a lighted window, but no other walkers. She would be in the second bedroom. Now the third.

She must have been crossing the landing when I approached the house on the opposite pavement. I tried to make my footsteps coincide with hers. Now she would be coming down the stairs, and the front door would open.

I deliberately did not look towards the house as a car came around the corner and moved towards me. I turned my head so that its lights would not shine on my face as it went by. But it did not go by. It stopped directly in front of the gate, and its lights went out. That was all. No slither of tyres or slamming of doors. Just a silent car at the kerbside.

It was at that moment that she chose to come out. I saw the door open, and I saw her turn to close it behind her. The light in the street was bad, but I think she was smiling, knowing that I would be watching as she came down the path.

She did not see Mr Miller get out of the car until it was far too late. He was a tall man and he had to stoop to unlatch the gate, but he did not have to hurry. There was nowhere for her to run.

I didn't see what happened next because I kept on walking. It was all I could do.

My father helped me then, although he never knew it. He ran his own computer business in the city, and my mother helped him in the shop, so neither of them were at home at that time of day. But Gary was, and that's where I went, and when I got there I invited him home with me. He came like a shot, as I knew he would, because my computer software was better than anything he could afford and I had this pretty good game which he was itching to get his hands on. It kept us busy for the next couple of hours while we were alone in the house, and I was able to plant a few ideas in his head about how long we'd been playing, so that in the end I was quite certain he'd have sworn we were together at the very time Dawn was in the Millers' house. Not that anyone ever asked him, or me. I was just taking out a bit of extra insurance. I knew I could rely on Dawn not to drag me in. She never did.

The train was rounding a curve, and the man glanced out of the window where the darkness seemed to be sliding by in the wrong direction as we began to slow.

'Manningtree,' he said. 'This is where I leave you.' He began to button his coat, but when he looked across the table for the last time he could see that I wanted to know more.

'She had to go away for a while, of course,' he said. 'But I did see her when they let her out. Not that we ever spoke again – it pays to be discreet, my friend.'

144

I could say nothing. The story, as far as he was concerned, had come to an end. Yet even he wanted to add something. 'She did find a way to let me know things were all right with her,' he said. 'One day we came face to face with each other in the corridor where she'd given me that note. She'd changed by this time, of course. There was no wildness in her at all, and she didn't say a word. She just held up her hand to show me that it had healed completely.' He edged into the gangway, smiling goodbye as the train came to rest. 'There was only one tiny scar in the middle of her palm. I was pleased about that.'

The guard's voice sounded over the moan of the idling engine. 'Manningtree,' it said. 'Manningtree. Passengers for the Hook of Holland change here.'

I caught one more glimpse of him. He was standing quite still on the bare platform, and I could not tell whether he had reached home or was soon to be on the deck of a ship sliding into the blackness of the night.

THE DELICATE SOUND
OF THUNDER

Brian Morse

'Thunder! Hate it. Always have. Ever since I was a kid. Used to cower under the bed when it thundered or lightning-ed. Delicate thunder? They can't ever have been in a thunderstorm.' I've never forgotten Ernie's first words. Looking back, how inapposite they seem! Thunder? No – fog was my undoing.

As I hauled myself up the two narrow metal steps into Ernie's cab the weight of the bag I was carrying tipped me forward over the seat and the case of the tape in my Walkman slid out of my pocket. I looked into a pair of eyes that searched me thoughtfully, too thoughtfully for my liking. 'What's this?' Ernie asked. He pounced on the cassette case. 'I like music.' I noticed how powerfully he was built.

'That? *The Delicate Sound of Thunder*,' I said. I put my hand out for the case. Suddenly I wished I'd looked more carefully before climbing in. I wasn't sure about him. But I'd been waiting an hour, hadn't I? I'd already turned down a lift from someone who'd obviously fancied his chances.

'Who's it by, then? Make yourself comfortable.'

'Pink Floyd.'

'I know. My brother-in-law's got records by him.' I didn't correct him. Then he told me his feelings about thunder. 'Student are you?' he asked. 'Never mind giving students lifts.'

I bet not, I thought, especially girl students. What was I doing taking the lift, then?

I said I was still at school, I'd been up to York with some friends, run out of money and had to get home as soon as possible. Without laying it on too thick I tried to make myself seem as young as possible. But at least he was going all the way back to the West Midlands. We discussed where he could drop me off so I could get home in one bus ride. There'd been nothing definite as yet, but I stayed wary of him. He told me about his job. It could have been worse. He could have talked about country-and-western, his passion in music.

Ernie must be getting on now. He seemed really old to me then, in his late forties at least. Still, back *then*, I was only sixteen and everyone over twenty-five seemed ancient, and I only spent a few hours with him.

One of the men up here at Caxby's got a really powerful portable radio – it gets VHF, medium wave, long wave, short, the lot. It took him years to wangle, but in due process of time, when all the forms had been filled in and sent off and pondered over by *them*, and double- and triple-stamped, then thought over again, it was brought up on the weekly supply run. Occasionally I borrow it. I go over the moor to the Hairpins. I listen mainly to local radio stations. They make me feel like I'm keeping in touch.

Then a couple of nights ago there I was, listening to Ernie! After all this time! Up till then I hadn't the faintest what had happened to him. For all I knew he could have been dead, and there he was on the radio!

I'm listening to Ernie now. Three nights in a row I've listened, three nights he's been on. It's been a different radio station each time, but from the suppressed sigh I know the DJ has already heard the story, maybe several times.

'This hitch-hiker I picked up,' he's saying. 'I don't know what her name was. There's a story I've got to tell. It's urgent someone listens. I've kept it to myself too long.'

'It's Ernie,' the DJ says, 'isn't it? Ernie from Wednesbury? Am I right? Tonight's topic for discussion is food additives and their effect on our health. Ernie, have you got anything to say about *that*?'

I laugh aloud. Poor man – landed with the nutter and the producer's gone off for coffee and no one to pull the plug.

'Food additives!' Ernie explodes. 'Who cares a damn!'

'Well, some people care a lot,' the DJ says sanctimoniously. 'How do you feel about mysterious substances being added to your food without your permission?'

'I've smoked fifty fags a day since I was ten,' Ernie says. 'That's some years I can tell you and I've never had a day off work. Food additives!'

So he's still working, still picking up hitch-hikers. Didn't his experience with me put him off? But how did he explain losing his pride and joy, his lorry, to his firm? Or did *they* do the explaining? Did *they* put things right for him to undermine the story he had to tell?

'Have you a point to make, Ernie?' the DJ says. You stupid old git, he's thinking. You nutter!

'Oh, I've a point all right,' Ernie says. 'The trouble is nobody'll believe me. Nobody'll believe the power government has. *They* only tolerate me, you know, because nobody believes me. If people did believe me they'd have me bumped off. But I've learnt to live with that. They've got my phone tapped, you know. One day you'll hear I had a motor accident in mysterious circumstances. Then you'll wish you listened.'

That's the trouble, isn't it, Ernie? Nobody will believe you. Even though what you say is true. And yes, certainly, they'll have your phone tapped. They'd be daft not to. Some day, somewhere, someone who matters and who's not in with them may start to pay attention. Then, oh yes, it'll be curtains for you.

'Okay, Ernie,' the DJ says. 'Let's have it. I'm giving you five minutes.' Maybe no one is queueing to talk about food additives, maybe he just fancies making a fool of Ernie. 'It's about the zombies again, is it?'

'Zombies!' Ernie explodes. 'What zombies? They were the lizard men! That's what they were!'

'Tell me from the beginning, Ernie,' the DJ says. 'I must have misunderstood about the zombies.' He suppresses a giggle.

'Lizard men. No one ever listens once I mention

150

them. Right. I picked up this hitch-hiker, a girl. Not far out of York.'

'What time of day was this?'

'Early evening. Dusk. Anyway, off we go. Then there's a traffic flash on the radio that there's been an accident on the A1, there's a ten-mile tailback and getting worse. I pulled into a lay-by to get the maps out— '

'And that's when you saw the lizard men, Ernie?'

Ernie soldiers on. 'I decided to go over the moors. Bit steep perhaps but there shouldn't have been much traffic about.'

'And was there?'

'A bit, not too bad. Then we ran into fog.'

We certainly did. You'd have taken the dark clouds up ahead for rain – and there'd been no mention of fog on the traffic flash – but suddenly we ran into a blank wall of it. There was a great hissing of air as Ernie braked the lorry. He swore.

'What's up?' I asked. I was sitting as close to the door as I could, my elbow resting on the handle. There'd been a moment in the lay-by where we'd pulled in to look at the map when I'd thought *this is it*. But the moment had passed.

'Fellow on our tail,' he said. 'Hanging on like grim death. Keeps poking his nose round my tail. Here he comes again!' There was something coming towards us at that moment. The car behind retreated. 'Don't teach patience nowadays,' Ernie grumbled.

The fog soon took us down to crawling speed. Every time it thinned out a bit the driver behind was encouraged to further efforts to overtake. He nearly killed himself half a dozen times in as many minutes. At last, though, he came zooming past. As he did so he hit another solid bank of fog. He swerved in front of us. Another vehicle's lights drilled towards us out of nowhere. Ernie swerved and braked so heavily I was thrown against the windscreen.

One second we were on the main road, following the vanishing rear lights of the car that had overtaken us, the next there was a tremendous thump at the front. It felt as if the lorry was flying. It was one of those moments when your whole life's supposed to flash in front of your eyes. The road had gone completely. Then, just as suddenly, we hit firm road surface again. The brakes screeched. I got the impression of sailing past a board like you get outside a factory. Cax-something. I couldn't read it properly.

'We must have ploughed through some roadworks,' Ernie shouted. 'I didn't see no sign though. I thought we'd hit a gate at first.'

Now I was peering through the windscreen again. 'It doesn't look like the road we were on,' I said doubtfully. Surely we were driving down a narrow lane? Had he done this on purpose?

'What?' Suddenly Ernie slowed the lorry down to a crawl. 'You're right. Doesn't look like our road at all.' He let the lorry run on for a hundred yards or so then stopped. 'Maybe it was a gate,' he said. 'A gate to a farm track.' *Not* a farm, I thought, remembering the glimpse of sign I'd seen. I tried to calm myself. He hadn't intended to come down here. Then he pulled on his handbrake. My heart thumped.

'What are you doing?' I said.

'Getting out to see if I can turn round. Want to come?'

I got out too. It was cold, an icy drizzle mixed in with the fog. This road we were on was hardly wider than the lorry. The verges on either side were a sodden quagmire.

Ernie's voice boomed, 'No chance of turning it round here.'

'It doesn't look like this road's been used in years,' I said. Though I saw straight away I was wrong. There were some quite recent tyre tracks. To the right, not very far away, you could hear the murmur of traffic on the main road.

'Why not back it up?' I suggested. 'I could guide you.'

Ernie laughed. 'Look!' he said, taking my shoulders. 'Didn't you notice you were in an articulated?' In the fog you couldn't see the rear. I shifted away from Ernie, those too easy hands.

'All the same— '

'Forget it!' Ernie said. 'I wouldn't risk backing in this marsh in daylight.' He walked down the nearside and called, 'They ain't going to like this back at the works. You seen these scratches? Whatever we hit was pretty solid.'

'Maybe I should go back to the main road and phone.'

'Phone!' he said. 'I haven't seen a house, let alone a phone box, the past five miles.' He took my arm and guided me towards the cab. Did he know how nervous of him I was? Did he like it?

*

153

'So you were on this farm track in the fog,' the DJ says. 'And you couldn't turn. Is that right, Ernie? Have I got it straight?'

'A real pea-souper,' Ernie says, 'like they used to get in Brum when I was a kid. And it wasn't a farm track. But I'll tell you about that in a minute. Anyhow, I drove on expecting there to be somewhere to turn, but there wasn't. Then the road started to go up and suddenly I found myself with an articulated going up a series of bends like those hairpins you get in the Alps. I managed three bends but on the fourth I stuck. I shouted to the hitch-hiker to get out and look.'

I jumped out as Ernie had told me. Close? The wheels of the main body of the lorry were only inches from the edge of the road. What the drop below was like I could only imagine – I ran back and made him come and see for himself. 'We'll *have* to move it,' he said, nearly beside himself. 'Christ! What if something comes? For God's sake, listen carefully. I'll show you exactly what I'm going to do.' He manhandled me into position. 'Stay there so I can see you in the mirror. Don't move!' If he'd had any designs on me in the lay-by, he didn't have now. He was too anxious about his lorry.

I stood where he'd put me. Then I heard a noise from above. A helicopter? Not very probable in this weather. The noise came closer and closer. When I realised what it was I ran back the length of the lorry and pounded on the cab door.

'Flag it down,' Ernie shouted. 'Stop them! Don't argue, girl!'

154

The vehicle was coming closer and closer. I could even see its shape above us now. There was no time to remind him there was no way another vehicle could get past anyway. I ran uphill frantically. The vehicle came slithering and sliding round the bend ahead of me with a squeal, then began to straighten out. But the driver seemed to have no intention of stopping. In fact he accelerated at me. I stopped dead. The vehicle – it seemed like an outsized jeep – at the last second skirted past me. The rush of air nearly knocked me over. There was no room for it to get past the lorry. It bounced off the trailer's side, then went over the edge. A few seconds later there was a sickening crunch.

Ernie clambered out of the cab. 'It had no headlights on,' he said with a kind of awe. 'Did you see the speed they were travelling? I thought they were going to run you down. In this weather with no lights on! What the hell were they playing at?'

'And what did you find down the bottom of the hill, Ernie?' the DJ asks. I'm not sure he believes a word of it. 'I can give you two more minutes.'

'It took us ages to find the vehicle,' Ernie says. 'Why it didn't set on fire I don't know. There was this terrible smell of petrol mixed in with the fog. We were ankle-deep in mud. You couldn't see a thing, not even my wagon up on the hairpins – I'd left the warning lights flashing. Then we found it. It was an army jeep. It was completely smashed. Mangled. No one could have survived.'

The DJ sounds a little more interested. Perhaps the producer's told him to pep it up. 'I suppose you checked?'

155

'I managed to get one of the doors off,' Ernie says. 'The man just tumbled out. The man on the other side, the driver, the wheel had gone through his chest. But the worst thing was the way they were dressed.'

'Two dead men and you're worrying about the way they're dressed?' the DJ says. 'Are you that fashion-conscious?'

'On a moor a million miles from anywhere, I come across two men dressed in silvery plastic suits like spacemen— '

'They could have been wearing some kind of insulating garment,' the DJ answers him back. He seems instinctively to dislike Ernie. 'You said they were army, didn't you? They could have been testing it out, couldn't they? You said it was late October. The army don't do these things in public, do they? You were obviously on one of their ranges.'

'And wearing breathing apparatus too?' Ernie says. 'What the hell for? We'd stumbled on something. It scared me silly. I didn't know what we'd got into – missiles, nuclear stuff, I didn't know what.'

'Right, your lorry's stuck on a hairpin, you've just caused an accident that's killed two men driving around without lights in spacemen suits,' the DJ says. 'What did you do then, Ernie? I know what I'd have done. I'd have hightailed it back to the main road and got the hell out of there. Is that what you did?'

'No,' Ernie says. He almost whispers. 'We went on.'

The DJ whistles. 'Why's that?'

'The hitch-hiker,' Ernie says. He pauses so my hand hovers over the volume knob ready to turn it up. I think he's going to ring off. Then he says,

'She misunderstood my motives. She thought I meant something towards her.'

We went back to the lorry. The situation was bad. Ernie didn't know what to do. The slightest mistake and the lorry would slip over the edge. But I had a decision of my own to make – to stick with him or not. Did I want to get involved in this? The two dead soldiers in their silvery suits had scared me stiff as well as him.

'Bloody army!' he kept muttering. 'Play damn-fool games in the dark and call them exercises. Do you know how many men get killed a year on so-called exercises? And them suits – what were they wearing them for? To practise invading the moon?'

He got up in the cab and began gathering things together. I could have just run into the fog. He'd never have caught me. Even if he was as strong as an ox he wasn't built for running.

He got back down and pushed his door to, very carefully so as not to rock the wagon. Then I remembered—

'My bag, Ernie.'

'You get it,' he snapped. 'I'm worn out.'

I clambered up the two steps and tugged at the nearside door. I couldn't get it open. 'Ernie . . . '

'Hell!' he said. Without waiting for me to get down he began to clamber up too. He squashed against me as he tried to release the handle.

'Get off!' I said. I felt crushed, humiliated.

'Now hang on, sweetheart!' he said. 'Don't get— '

The 'sweetheart' did it. 'Get off!' I screamed.

'I'm a married man,' he said. 'I've got daughters

your age.' He tried to pull himself up the extra step.
I shoved him down to the road. It was a long way.

'Misunderstood you? I see . . . ' The DJ pauses.
'So what did you do when the girl ran off, then,
Ernie?' He's forgotten about lizard men and zombies
and soldiers in silver suits. I can tell he's sensing a
different sort of story altogether.

'Why, followed her of course! When I got my
wind back. I couldn't just leave her in the middle
of a wilderness!'

'Where you took her!'

'By accident! Now, look here— '

'Sorry, Ernie. I didn't mean anything. But which
way did she go?'

'Uphill. Up the rest of the bends.'

'And did you fancy her, Ernie?' the DJ says out of
the blue, doing his shock-tactic psychiatrist-detective
bit.

'What's that got to do with it?'

'Long-distance lorry drivers do have a certain
reputation.'

Ernie takes a long time to answer. 'Okay, I
did fancy her. Anyone would. She was lovely. But
I didn't give her cause to be scared. Maybe in the
past I might have— '

'The past, Ernie? You have a past?'

'We've all got pasts. I've never done anything to
be ashamed of,' Ernie says passionately. 'I wouldn't
do anything to anyone who didn't want me to.'

'Okay, okay, Ernie,' the DJ says soothingly. 'But
this hitch-hiker girl. Where did you say she was from?
Tell me that.'

158

'Walsall. Down towards Hill Top she said.'

'How long ago's this?' There's an edge to the DJ's voice.

'Five years,' Ernie says. 'But I haven't finished the story.'

'And what was she like?' the DJ insists. 'Describe her. Come on, Ernie. You seem to have a very good memory.'

'Short, five foot two. Long blonde hair. Bluey eyes. Slim.'

'Sounds like a dream. Was she wearing anything special?'

'Jeans, anorak, the usual sort of thing. Oh – the anorak. A pinky colour it was – cerise she called it. That's what made me stop to pick her up. Really stuck out it did. A ski jacket she said it was. What do you want to know all that for?'

'Hang on, Ernie,' the DJ says breathlessly, as if he's just rushed back to the microphone. 'You'll have to be patient with me for a moment. We've got a little technical problem.'

'Hello! Hello! Are you there?' Ernie shouts.

There's silence on the radio, a full thirty seconds, then the DJ comes back. 'Sorry about that, Ernie. Go on with your story. I'm interested, very interested. All our listeners are.'

Suddenly, with a shock of realisation, I see what the DJ's up to. And suddenly I wonder, for the first time ever – could I have misjudged Ernie that night? And then I think, fleetingly – if Ernie could see me now he wouldn't think how pretty I am.

*

Up on the very top that night there was a breeze which blew gaps in the fog. Strange shapes seemed to loom through it, but I was more scared of Ernie than phantasms. If only I'd run the other way. But his sprawling body had been in my path. I'd been afraid he'd grab at my ankles as I ran past. Now I was scared I'd hurt him badly and he'd be out for my blood.

The road began to go gently down. I slowed to a trot, then stopped altogether. No sign of Ernie. I walked on, glancing over my shoulder all the time. Maybe I'd hurt him badly. Maybe I ought to go back and help him. Then I heard the sound of water and suddenly I walked out of the fog into clear night and a starry sky. Ahead were the lights of a small village. I hurried again. I didn't want Ernie to catch up when I was so close to safety. Never had I wanted to be anywhere as badly as I wanted to be in that village.

A little bridge in a hollow took me over a stream, and here the road forked. I stopped. Which way? Then on the path to the right I saw two figures with a dog. Behind me I heard Ernie coming, shouting and running down towards me like a maniac. With all the strength I had left I ran towards the men. As I did so a figure appeared from off the moor, splashed through the stream and stopped them.

'So you saw this figure in the mist when you were chasing after the girl hitch-hiker,' the DJ says to Ernie. 'You're sure you don't remember her name?' he adds, to catch him off his guard.

'I told you. She never said.'

'And it wasn't marked in her bag or anywhere like that?'

'I never saw inside her bag, never touched it,' Ernie says. 'I thought you wanted me to finish my story? A quarter of an hour ago I was wasting your precious air-time.'

'This figure in the mist, then,' the DJ says soothingly.

'It looked like a tramp,' Ernie says. 'All muffled up and wrapped up against the weather.'

'A tramp in the middle of the moor? Bit odd, wasn't it? Car spotting, was he?' The DJ can't resist the sarcasm.

'I didn't stop to think what he was doing. There were two dead men and my lorry stuck and this girl running away from me because she'd misjudged my intentions. He shouted something at me about not going any further, I should turn back.'

'Why didn't you?'

'You know why.'

'And then?' the DJ prompts.

'The fog stopped, like a line drawn across the moor. I could see a village about a mile ahead. The girl was standing at the bottom just over a bridge. I ran like hell.'

'Why was that? To stop her? Scared of what she'd say when she got to the village, were you?'

'No! A thousand times no! I could see this tramp, as I thought he was, running hell for leather across the moor to cut her off. I screamed to her to stop, to watch out for him, but when she heard me she just took off again. And then there were two other men coming in her direction along another path. With a dog. She must have thought she'd be safe with them.'

*

161

I was only a few yards from those men when I sensed something was wrong. It was the way they were dressed, all muffled up, hooded, almost like monks. A crazy idea shot through my mind – that I'd stumbled into the grounds of a monastery, that I shouldn't be there because I was a woman.

'You! Stop! You!' one of them shouted. The dog rushed and yapped at my feet. Ernie was screaming behind me. 'Go back to your friend,' the man shouted. 'You're almost over the boundary.'

Boundary? What was he talking about? I ran on to the grass and tried to skirt round them. I wanted the village. I wanted the police. I didn't want Ernie.

The man ran after me and caught me up in a few strides. I stopped abruptly and turned. We almost bumped into each other. He didn't grab me, though, or even attempt to touch me. 'Go back,' he said. 'Whatever you're scared of. Anything's better than this.' His voice was very gentle.

His eyes glistened inside the hood. I was drawn to them, they were shining so brightly. I leant forward to draw the hood aside. His hand came up to stop me, but too late. I'd already touched the cloth. I yanked it aside.

'I knew why she'd screamed. They were inhuman,' Ernie said. 'They had skins like lizards. They sounded all right, they looked all right, but when their hoods were off – I can't describe it. I did what they told me. I went back. I left her. That I can't forgive myself for.'

*

The man who'd tried to stop me gave up the chase when I reached the village street. I saw him stop outside the circuit of the first light. I was gasping and crying to myself. I thought I'm safe now. He doesn't want to be seen, whatever.

Through the window of a house I saw a family gathered round a television. In another house a family was sitting down to the evening meal. They were eating by candle-light. How charming, how olde worlde, I thought. In another house someone was playing a piano. Here was civilisation indeed!

I hurried up the street. There was a pub ahead. I found the energy to run again through its small car park, into the porch. There was laughter inside. I lifted the latch and stepped inside.

For a moment no one noticed me, then every voice stopped. The entire pub turned towards me and stared. The barman suddenly turned too and lifted the needle off the record.

Lizard men.

My pursuer had very quietly come up behind me. I turned to face him. He pulled his hood off.

'We convinced your friend,' he said. 'He's gone back. But you . . . ' He touched my face. 'You ran into the infected ground. You'll have to stay.'

'Ever heard of an Elizabeth Turner who went missing near York about the time you're talking about, Ernie?' the DJ's saying. The police computer must have yielded my name. 'She was from Hill Top. She answers the description you gave.'

'Elizabeth?' Ernie says dully. 'Was she called that?

163

She never came out of that place. I know. I waited two days by the gates I'd run through. I watched them bring out my lorry . . . '

Two soldiers on supply-run to the germ establishment where an experiment had gone horribly wrong ten years before, under standing orders not to show any lights on their vehicles in case the public saw and asked questions, naturally thought the lorry blocking their path was a trap. But they'd already been careless. They'd not properly closed the gate off the main road.

They paid for it. Now, it seems, Ernie's going to pay for it too.

No way I can warn you, Ernie. We've no phones up here, no way of communicating with the outside world. No doubt, one day, when all of us lizard people are dead, and it's not worth suppressing the story any longer, everything will come out.

By now they've probably traced your number, the police car is probably already drawing up outside your front gate.

Can you be charged with murder when there's no body?

'I don't know what happened to her, what was wrong up at that place, but it swallowed her alive. I stayed there two days and waited. I bought that record she was listening to, though. My wife thought I was barmy!'

'What was that?' the DJ asks. He'd like a full confession. Location of the body et cetera. 'What record?'

'*The Delicate Sound of Thunder*. I've still got it somewhere. Perhaps I'll get it out now I've had the courage to tell someone about – you know what. Thank you for letting me talk. I loved that girl.' He pauses, then laughs. 'I still can't fathom how thunder can be delicate though.' He puts the phone down.

'Ernie!' the DJ shouts, 'Ernie! Ernie! . . . Damn you!'

It thunders up here often. I wouldn't call the sound of thunder delicate either, Ernie.

I hope you put the phone down soon enough.

Ouida Sebestyen
The Girl in the Box £2.99

Nobody comes, and I'm down here, wherever that is, I'm here by myself, locked in and so confused I'm not thinking straight . . .

'In a portrait of a teenager trapped by mysterious circumstances – Sebestyen has written an extraordinary thriller . . . Like Anne Frank, Jacklyn McGee's courage and humanity shine through her self-revelation. A story that's impossible to put down' KIRKUS REVIEWS

Ann McPherson and Aidan Macfarlane
Me and My Mates £2.99

"I hate parties. I worry non-stop about what they're going to be like for hours ahead."

But this one was something else.

If Steve and his mates had known in advance how wild this scene was going to turn out, they'd have worried one hell of a lot more. Tony started it. He always did. His brew nearly blasted out their braincells. For Steve, Rachel, Jerry, David and Miranda it was a night they were never to forget.

Not that they'd all make it in the end.

Jim Naughton
My Brother Stealing Second £3.50

Stealing second is baseball talk, and Bobby loved baseball and his brother Billy more than anything. But Billy is dead, killed in a car crash, and everything in Bobby's life has changed. He knows he's in a mess, but does it really matter any more?

Two things show him it does: the beautiful Annie Dunham, whose parents died in the same crash, and the incredible truth about what really happened that night. At last, he knows exactly what he's got to do ...

'Naughton hits a home run on every page ... *My Brother Stealing Second* is a grand-slam book' THE WASHINGTON POST

Will Gatti
Absolute Trust £3.50

The Bureau of Internal Affairs August 6, 1999

To: All Agents Confidential

Suspect arrives Heathrow, 1200 GMT. Full surveillance authorised.

Britain was no longer the place for an easy holiday. These days people disappeared there. And elections and free speech were a thing of the past.

Not that Jeremiah Talent was worried. He was smart. People liked him. And besides, didn't everyone know that his father was the US Ambassador?

But the wrong people had heard about Jeremiah Talent.

And now they were going to teach him a thing or two about fear ...

All Pan books are available at your local bookshop or newsagent, or can be ordered direct from the publisher. Indicate the number of copies required and fill in the form below.

Send to: **CS Department, Pan Books Ltd., P.O. Box 40, Basingstoke, Hants. RG21 2YT.**

or phone: 0256 469551 (Ansaphone), quoting title, author and Credit Card number.

Please enclose a remittance* to the value of the cover price plus: 60p for the first book plus 30p per copy for each additional book ordered to a maximum charge of £2.40 to cover postage and packing.

*Payment may be made in sterling by UK personal cheque, postal order, sterling draft or international money order, made payable to Pan Books Ltd.

Alternatively by Barclaycard/Access:

Card No.

Signature:

Applicable only in the UK and Republic of Ireland.

While every effort is made to keep prices low, it is sometimes necessary to increase prices at short notice. Pan Books reserve the right to show on covers and charge new retail prices which may differ from those advertised in the text or elsewhere.

NAME AND ADDRESS IN BLOCK LETTERS PLEASE:

....

Name —————————————————————————————

Address —————————————————————————————

—————————————————————————————

—————————————————————————————

—————————————————————————————

3/87